ENJOY FOUR NOVELS AND
ONE COLLECTION OF STORIES
FEATURING THE MASTER
ENCHANTER CHRESTOMANCI

CHARMED LIFE

Winner of England's Guardian Award
Commended for the Carnegie Medal
An ABA "Pick of the Lists"

"A charming fantasy with a fresh twist and
real humor. . . . An outstanding success."
—Andre Norton

THE LIVES OF CHRISTOPHER CHANT

An ALA Notable Book
A Nebula Award Nominee

"A perfectly self-sufficient classic-to-be in
the irresistible genre of stories about mysterious passages, treasures, or verdant places
hidden behind the walls of old houses."
—*The Washington Post Book World*

THE MAGICIANS OF CAPRONA

"A wicked enchanter is at work undermining the charms which once defended [Caprona] from its foes. . . . A gorgeous concoction of humor, suspense, and romance." —*The Horn Book*

WITCH WEEK

A *School Library Journal* Best Book of the Year

"This is a remarkably adroit blending of vivid fantasy, a funny and perceptive school story, and a thoughtful commentary on how thin the line is that separates what is from what might be."
  —*The Bulletin of the Center for Children's Books*
                    (starred review)

MIXED MAGICS: FOUR TALES OF CHRESTOMANCI

"A new addition to the Chrestomanci canon is cause for celebration."
                    —*The Horn Book*

Diana Wynne Jones
Mixed Magics

A Greenwillow Book

HarperTrophy®
An Imprint of HarperCollins*Publishers*

"Warlock at the Wheel" was first published in *Warlock at the Wheel and Other Stories* by
Diana Wynne Jones, Macmillan Children's Books. © 1984 Diana Wynne Jones.

"Stealer of Souls" was first published in *Mixed Magics* by Diana Wynne Jones,
Collins. © 2000 Diana Wynne Jones.

"Carol Oneir's Hundredth Dream" was first published in *Dragons & Dreams*, edited
by Jane Yolen, Martin H. Greenberg, and Charles G. Waugh, Harper & Row.
© 1986 by Diana Wynne Jones.

"The Sage of Theare" was first published in *Hecate's Cauldron*, edited by Susan M.
Schwartz, DAW Books. © 1982 Diana Wynne Jones.

Mixed Magics
Copyright © 2000 by Diana Wynne Jones

Library of Congress Cataloging-in-Publication Data
Jones, Diana Wynne.
Mixed magics : four tales of Chrestomanci / by Diana Wynne Jones.
p.   cm.
"Greenwillow Books."
Summary: Four separate incidents test the power of the Chrestomanci, a powerful
enchanter with nine lives, to control misuses of magic on various worlds.
ISBN 0-06-029705-0 — ISBN 0-06-029706-9 (lib. bdg.)
ISBN 0-06-441018-8 (pbk.)
[1. Fantasy. 2. Magic—Fiction.] I. Title.
PZ7.J684 Mi 2001   00-062277
[Fic]—dc21   CIP
                                                                    AC

❖
First Harper Trophy edition, 2003
Visit us on the World Wide Web!
www.harperchildrens.com

THERE ARE THOUSANDS of worlds, all different from ours. Chrestomanci's world is the one next door to us, and the difference here is that magic is as common as music is with us. It is full of people working magic—warlocks, witches, thaumaturges, sorcerers, fakirs, conjurers, hexers, magicians, mages, shamans, diviners, and many more—from the lowest Certified witch right up to the most powerful of enchanters. Enchanters are strange as well as powerful. Their magic is different and stronger, and many of them have more than one life.

Now, if someone did not control all these busy magic users, ordinary people would have a horrible time and probably end up as slaves. So the government appoints the very strongest enchanter there is to make sure no one misuses magic. This enchanter has nine lives and is known as the Chrestomanci. You pronounce it KREST-OH-MAN-SEE. He has to have a strong personality as well as strong magic.

—Diana Wynne Jones

MIXED MAGICS

CONTENTS

WARLOCK AT THE WHEEL

*T*HE WILLING WARLOCK was a born loser. He lost his magic when Chrestomanci took it away, and that meant he lost his usual way of making a living. So he decided to take up a life of crime instead by stealing a motorcar, because he loved motorcars, and selling it. He found a beautiful car in Wolvercote High Street, but he lost his head when a policeman saw him trying to pick the lock and cycled up to know what he was doing. He ran.

The policeman pedaled after him, blowing his whistle, and the Willing Warlock climbed over the nearest wall and ran again, with the whistle still sounding, until he arrived in the backyard of a onetime Accredited Witch who was a friend of his. "What shall I do?" he panted.

"How should I know?" said the Accredited

Witch. "I'm not used to doing without magic any more than you are. The only soul I know who's still in business is a French wizard in Shepherd's Bush."

"Tell me his address," said the Willing Warlock.

The Accredited Witch told him. "But it won't do you a scrap of good," she said unhelpfully. "Jean-Pierre always charges the earth. Now I'll thank you to get out of here before you bring the police down on me, too."

The Willing Warlock went out of the witch's front door into Coven Street and blenched at the sound of police whistles still shrilling in the distance. Since it seemed to him that he had no time to waste, he hurried to the nearest toyshop and parted with his last half crown for a toy pistol. Armed with this, he walked into the first post office he came to.

"Your money or your life," he said to the postmistress. The Willing Warlock was a bulky young man who always looked as if he needed to shave, and the Postmistress was sure he was a desperate character. She let him clear out her safe.

The Willing Warlock put the money and the pistol in his pocket and hailed a taxi in which he drove all the way to Shepherd's Bush, feeling this was the next best thing to having a car of his own. It cost a lot, but he arrived at the French wizard's office still with £273 6s 4d in his pocket.

The French wizard shrugged in a very French way. "What is it you expect me to do for you, my friend? Me, I try not to offend the police. If you wish me to help, it will cost you."

"A hundred pounds," said the Willing Warlock. "Hide me somehow."

Jean-Pierre did another shrug. "For that money," he said, "I could hide you two ways. I could turn you into a small round stone—"

"No, thanks," said the Willing Warlock.

"—and keep you in a drawer," said Jean-Pierre. "Or I could send you to another world entirely. I could even send you to a world where you would have your magic again—"

"Have my magic?" exclaimed the Willing Warlock.

"—but that would cost you twice as much," said Jean-Pierre. "Yes, naturally you could have your magic again, if you went somewhere where Chrestomanci has no power. The man is not all-powerful."

"Then I'll go to one of those places," said the

Willing Warlock.

"Very well." In a bored sort of way, Jean-Pierre picked up a pack of cards and fanned them out. "Choose a card. This decides which world you will grace with your blue chin."

As the Willing Warlock stretched out his hand to take a card, Jean-Pierre moved them out of reach. "Whatever world it is," he said, "the money there will be quite different from your pounds, shillings, and pence. You might as well give me all you have."

So the Willing Warlock handed over all his £273 6s 4d. Then he was allowed to pick a card. It was the ten of clubs. Not a bad card, the Willing Warlock thought. He was no fortune-teller, of course, but he knew the ten of clubs meant that someone would bully somebody. He decided that he would be the one doing the bully-ing, and handed back the card. Jean-Pierre tossed all the cards carelessly down on a table. The Willing Warlock just had time to see that every single one was the ten of clubs, before he found himself still in Shepherd's Bush but in another world entirely.

He was standing in what seemed to be a car park beside a big road. On that road, more cars than he had ever seen in his life were rushing past, together with lorries and the occasional big red bus. There were cars standing all around him. This was a good world indeed!

The Willing Warlock sniffed the delicious smell of petrol and turned to the nearest parked car to see how it worked. It looked rather different from the one he had tried to steal in Wolvercote. Experimentally he made a magic pass over its bonnet. To his delight, the bonnet promptly sprang open an inch or so. The French wizard had not lied. He had his magic back.

The Willing Warlock was just about to heave up the bonnet and plunge into the mysteries beneath when he saw a large lady in uniform, with a yellow band around her cap, tramping meaningfully toward him. She must be a policewoman. Now he had his magic back, the Willing Warlock did not panic. He simply let go of the bonnet and sauntered casually away. Rather to his surprise, the policewoman did not follow him. She just gave him a look of deep contempt and tucked a message of some kind behind the wiper of the car.

All the same, the Willing Warlock felt it prudent to go on walking. He walked to another street, looking at cars all the time, until something made him look up. In front of him was a grand marble building. CITY BANK, it said, in rich gold letters. Now here, thought the Willing Warlock, was a better way to get a car than simply stealing it. If he robbed this bank, he could buy a car of his very own. He took the toy pistol out of his pocket and went in through the grand door.

Inside, it was very hushed and polite and calm. Though there were quite a lot of people there, waiting in front of the cashiers or walking about in the background, nobody seemed to notice the Willing Warlock standing uncertainly waving his pistol. He was forced to go and push the nearest queue of people aside and point the pistol at the lady behind the glass there.

"Money or your life," he said.

They seemed to notice him then. Somebody screamed. The lady behind the glass went white and put her thumb on a button near her cash drawer. "How—how much money, sir?" she faltered.

"All of it," said the Willing Warlock. "Quickly." Maybe, he thought afterward, that was a bit greedy. But it seemed so easy. Everyone, on both sides of the glassed-in counter, was standing frozen, staring at him, afraid of the pistol. And the lady readily opened her cash drawer and began counting out wads of five-pound notes, fumbling with haste and eagerness.

While she was doing it, the door of the bank opened and someone came in. The Willing Warlock glanced over his shoulder and saw it was only a small man in a pin-striped suit, who seemed to be staring like everybody else. The lady was actually passing the Willing Warlock the first bundle of money when the small man shouted out in a very big voice, "Don't be a fool! He's only joking. That's a toy pistol!"

At once everyone near turned on the Willing Warlock. Three men tried to grab him. An old lady swung her handbag and clouted him around the head. "Take that, you thief!" A bell began to ring loudly. And, worse still, an unholy howling started somewhere outside, coming closer and closer. "That's the police coming!" screamed the old lady, and she went for the Willing Warlock again.

The Willing Warlock turned and ran, with everyone trying to stop him and getting in his way. The last person who got in his way was the small man in the pin-striped suit. He took hold of the Willing Warlock's sleeve and said, "Wait a minute—"

The Willing Warlock was so desperate by then that he fired the toy pistol at him. A stream of water came out of it and caught the small man in one eye, drenching his smart suit. The small man ducked and let go. The Willing Warlock burst out through the door of the bank.

The howling outside was hideous. It was coming from a white car labeled POLICE, with a blue flashing light on top, which was racing down the street toward him. There was rather a nice car parked by the curb, facing toward the police car. A big, shiny, expensive car. Even in his panic, and as he wondered how the police had been fetched so quickly, that car caught the Willing Warlock's eye. As the police car screamed to a stop and policemen started to jump out of it, the Willing Warlock tore open the door of the nice car, jumped into the seat behind the steering wheel, and set it going in a burst of desperate magic.

Behind him, the policemen jumped back into their car, which then did a screaming U-turn and came after him. The Willing Warlock saw them coming in a little mirror somebody had thoughtfully fixed to the windscreen. He flung the nice car around a corner out of sight. But the police car followed. The Willing Warlock screamed around another corner, and another. But the police car stuck to him like a leech.

The Willing Warlock realized that he had better spare a little magic from making the car go in order to make the car look different. So as he screamed around yet another corner into the main road he had first seen, he put out his last ounce of magic and turned the car bright pink. To his relief, the police car went past him and roared away into the distance.

The Willing Warlock relaxed a little. He had a nice car of his own now and he seemed to be safe for the moment. But he still had to learn how to make the thing go properly, instead of by magic, and as he soon discovered, there seemed to be all sorts of other rules to driving that he had never even imagined.

For one thing, all the cars kept to the left-hand side, and motorists seemed to get very annoyed when they found a large pink car coming toward them on the other side of the road. Then there were some streets where all the cars seemed to be coming toward the pink car, and the people in those cars shook their fists and pointed and hooted at the Willing Warlock. Then again, sometimes there were lights at crossroads, and people did not seem to like you going past them when they were red.

The Willing Warlock was not very clever, but he did realize quite soon that cars were not often pink. A pink car that broke all these rules was bound to be noticed. So while he drove on and on, looking for some quiet street where he could learn how the car really worked, he sought about for some other way to disguise the car. He saw that all cars had a plate in front and behind, with letters and numbers on. That made it easy.

He changed the front number plate to WW100 and the back one to XYZ123 and let the car return to its nice shiny gray color and drove soberly on till he found some back streets lined with quiet houses. By this time he was quite tired. He had never had much magic, and he was out of practice anyway. He was glad to stop and look for the knob that made the engine go.

There were rows of knobs, but none of them seemed to be the one he wanted. One knob squirted water all over the front window. Another opened the side windows and brought wet, windy air sighing in. Another flashed lights. Yet another made a loud hooting, which made the Willing Warlock jump. People would notice!

He became panicky and found his neck going hot and cold in gusts, with a specially cold, panicky spot in the middle, at the back, just above his collar. He tried another knob. That played music. The next knob made voices speak. "Over and out . . . Yes. Pink. I don't know how he got a respray that quick, but it's definitely him . . ."

The Willing Warlock, in even more of a panic, realized he was listening to the police by magic, and that they were still hunting him. In his panic he pressed another knob, which made wipers start furiously waving across the windscreen, wiping off the water the first knob had squirted.

"Doh!" said the Willing Warlock, and put up his hand irritably to rub that panicky cold spot at the back of his neck.

The cold place was connected to a long, warm, hairy muzzle. Whatever owned the muzzle objected to being wiped away. It let out a deep bass growl and a blast of warm, smelly air.

The Willing Warlock snatched his hand away. In his terror, he pressed another button, which caused the seat he was in to collapse gently backward until he was lying on his back. He found himself staring up into the face of the largest dog he had ever seen. It was a great pepper-colored brute, with white fangs to match the size of the rest of it. Evidently he had stolen a dog as well as a car.

"Grrrrr," repeated the dog. It bent its great head until the noise vibrated the Willing Warlock's skull like a road drill, and sniffed his face loudly.

"Get off," said the Willing Warlock tremulously.

Worse followed. Something surged in the backseat beside the huge dog. A small, shrill voice, sounding very sleepy, said, "Why have we stopped for, Daddy?"

"Oh, my *gawd!*" said the Willing Warlock. He turned his eyes gently sideways under the great dog's face. Sure enough, there was a child on the backseat beside the dog, a rather small child with reddish hair and a slobbery, sleepy face.

"You're not my daddy," this child said accusingly.

The Willing Warlock rather liked children on the whole, but he knew he would have to get rid of this one somehow. To steal a car and a dog and a child would probably put him in prison for life. People really did not like you stealing children.

Frantically he reached forward and pushed

knobs. Lights lit, wipers swatted and unswatted, voices spoke, a hooter sounded, but at last he pushed the right one, and the seat rose gracefully upright again. He used his magic on the rear door, and it sprang open.

"Out," he said. "Both of you. Get out and wait, and your daddy will find you."

Dog and child turned and stared at the open door. Their faces, puzzled and slightly indignant, turned back to the Willing Warlock. It was their car, after all.

The Willing Warlock tried a bit of coaxing. "Get out. Nice dog. Good boy."

"Grrrr," said the dog, and the child said, "I'm not a boy."

"I meant the dog," the Willing Warlock said hastily. The dog's growl enlarged to a rumble that shook the car. Perhaps the dog was not a boy either. The Willing Warlock knew when he was beaten. It was a pity, when it was such a nice car, but this world was full of cars. Provided he made sure the next one was empty, he could steal one anytime he liked. He slammed the rear door shut and started to open his own.

The dog was too quick for him. Before he had reached the handle, its great teeth were fastened into the shoulder of his jacket, right through the cloth. He could feel them digging into his skin underneath. And it growled harder than ever. "Let go," the Willing Warlock said, without hope, and sat very still.

"Go on driving," commanded the child.

"Why?" said the Willing Warlock.

"Because I like driving in cars," said the child. "Towser will let you go when you drive."

"I don't know how to make the car go," the Willing Warlock said sullenly.

"Stupid," said the child. "Daddy uses those keys there, and he pushes on the pedals with his feet."

Towser backed this up with another growl and dug his teeth in a little. Towser clearly knew his job, and his job seemed to be to back up anything the child said. The Willing Warlock sighed, thinking of years in prison, but he found the keys and located the pedals. He turned the keys. He pushed on the pedals. The engine started with a roar.

Then another voice spoke. "You have forgotten to fasten your seat belt," it said. "I cannot proceed until you do so."

It was here that the Willing Warlock realized that his troubles had only just begun. The car was bullying him now. He had no idea where the seat belt was, but it is amazing what you can do if a mouthful of white fangs are fastened into your shoulder. The Willing Warlock found the seat belt. He did it up. He found a lever that said "forward" and pushed it. He pressed on pedals. The engine roared, but nothing else happened.

"You are wasting petrol," the car told him acidly. "Release the hand brake. I cannot pro—"

The Willing Warlock found a sort of stick in the floor and moved it. It snapped like a crocodile, and the car jerked. "You are wasting petrol," the car said, boringly. "Release the foot brake. I cannot proceed—"

Luckily, since Towser was growling even louder than the car, the Willing Warlock took his left foot off a pedal first. They shot off down the road. "You are wasting petrol," the car told him.

"Oh, shut up," the Willing Warlock said. But nothing shut the car up, he discovered, except not pressing so hard on the right-hand pedal.

Towser, on the other hand, seemed satisfied as soon as the car moved. He let go of the Willing Warlock and loomed behind him on the backseat, while the child sat and chanted, "Go on, go on, go on driving."

The Willing Warlock kept on driving. There is nothing else you can do if a child, a dog the size of Towser, and a car all combine to make you. At least the car was easy to drive. All the Willing Warlock had to do was sit there not pressing the pedal too much and keep turning into the emptiest streets. He had time to think. He knew the dog's name. If he could find out the child's name, then he could work a spell on them both to make them let him go.

"What's your name?" he asked, turning into a wide straight road with room for three cars abreast in it.

"Jemima Jane," said the child. "Go on, go on, go on driving."

The Willing Warlock drove, muttering a spell. While he did, Towser made a flowing sort of jump and landed in the passenger seat beside him, where he sat in a royal way, staring out at the road. The Willing Warlock cowered away from him and finished the spell in a gabble. The beast was as big as a lion!

"You are wasting petrol," remarked the car.

Perhaps these things caused the Willing Warlock to muddle the spell. All that happened was that Towser turned invisible.

There was an instant shriek from the backseat. "Where's Towser?"

The invisible space on the front passenger seat growled horribly. The Willing Warlock did not know where its teeth were. He hurriedly revoked the spell. Towser loomed beside him, looking reproachful.

"You're not to do that again!" said Jemima Jane.

"I won't if we all get out and walk," the Willing Warlock said cunningly.

A silence met this suggestion, with an undercurrent of snarl to it. The Willing Warlock gave up for the moment and kept on driving. There were no houses by the road anymore, only trees, grass, and a few cows, and the road stretched into the distance, endlessly. The nice gray car, labeled "WW100" in front and "XYZ123" behind, zoomed gently onward for nearly an hour. The sun began setting in gory clouds, behind some low green hills.

"I want my supper," announced Jemima Jane. At the word *supper*, Towser yawned and started to dribble. He turned to look thoughtfully at the Willing Warlock, obviously wondering which bits of him tasted best. "Towser's hungry, too," said Jemima Jane.

The Willing Warlock turned his eyes sideways to look at Towser's great pink tongue draped over Towser's large white fangs. "I'll stop at the first place we see," he said obligingly. He began turning over schemes for giving both of them—not to speak of the car—the slip the moment they allowed him to stop. If he made himself invisible, so that the dog could not find him—

He seemed to be in luck. Just then a large blue notice that said HARBURY SERVICES came into view, with a picture of a knife and fork underneath. The Willing Warlock turned into it with a squeal of tires. "You are wasting petrol," the car protested.

The Willing Warlock took no notice. He stopped with a jolt among a lot of other cars, turned himself invisible, and tried to jump out. But he had forgotten the seat belt. It held him in place long enough for Towser to fix his fangs in the sleeve of his coat, and that seemed to be enough to make Towser turn invisible, too. "You have forgotten to set the hand brake," said the car.

"Doh!" snarled the Willing Warlock miserably, and put the hand brake on. It was not easy, with Towser's invisible fangs grating his arm.

"You're to fetch me lots and lots," Jemima Jane

said. It did not seem to trouble her that both of them had vanished. "Towser, make sure he brings me an ice cream."

The Willing Warlock climbed out of the car, lugging the invisible Towser. He tried some more cunning. "Come with me and show me which ice cream you want," he called back. Several people in the car park looked around to see where the invisible voice was coming from.

"I want to stay in the car. I'm tired," whined Jemima Jane.

The invisible teeth fastened in the Willing Warlock's sleeve rumbled a little. Invisible dribble ran on his hand. "Oh, all right," he said, and set off for the restaurant, accompanied by four invisible heavy paws.

Maybe it was a good thing they were both invisible. There was a big sign on the door: NO DOGS. And the Willing Warlock still had no money. He went to the long counter and picked up pies and scones with the hand Towser left him free. He stuffed them into his pocket so that they would become invisible, too.

Someone pointed to the Danish pastry he picked up next and screamed, "Look! A ghost!" Then there were screams further down the counter. The Willing Warlock looked. A very large chocolate gâteau, with a snout-shaped piece missing from it, was trotting at chest level across the dining area. Towser was helping himself, too. People backed away, yelling. The gâteau broke into a gallop and barged out through the glass doors with a splat. At the same moment, someone grabbed the Danish pastry from the Willing Warlock's hand.

It was the girl behind the cash desk, who was not afraid of ghosts. "You're the Invisible Man or something," she said. "Give that back."

The Willing Warlock panicked again and ran after the gâteau. He meant to go on running, as fast as he could, in the opposite direction from the nice car. But as soon as he barged through the door, he found the gâteau waiting for him, lying on the ground. A warning growl and hot breath on his hand suggested that he pick the gâteau up and come along. Teeth in his trouser leg backed up this suggestion. Dismally, the Willing Warlock obeyed.

"Where's my ice cream?" Jemima Jane asked ungratefully.

"There wasn't any," said the Willing Warlock as Towser herded him into the car. He threw the gâteau, the scones, and a pork pie onto the back-seat. "Be thankful for what you've got."

"Why?" asked Jemima Jane.

The Willing Warlock gave up. He turned him-self visible again and sat in the driving seat to eat the other pork pie. He could feel Towser snuffing him from time to time to make sure he stayed there. In between, he could hear Towser eating. Towser made such a noise that the Willing Warlock was glad he was invisible. He looked to make sure. And there was Towser, visible again in all his huge-ness, sitting in the backseat licking his vast chops. As for Jemima Jane, the Willing Warlock had to look away quickly. She was chocolate all over. There was a river of chocolate down her front and more plastered into her red curls like mud.

"Why aren't you going on driving for?" Jemima Jane demanded. Towser at once surged to his huge feet to back up the demand.

"I am, I am!" the Willing Warlock said, hastily starting the engine.

"You have forgotten to fasten your seat belt," the car reminded him priggishly. And as the car moved forward, it added, "It is now lighting-up time. You require headlights."

The Willing Warlock started the wipers, rolled

down the windows, played music, and finally managed to turn on the lights. He drove back onto the big road, hating all three of them. And drove. Jemima Jane stood up on the backseat behind him. The gâteau had made her distressingly lively. She wanted to talk. She grabbed one of the Willing Warlock's ears in a sticky chocolate hand for balance and breathed gâteau fumes and questions into his other ear.

"Why did you take our car for? What are all those prickles on your chin for? Why don't you like me holding your nose for? Why don't you smell nice? Where are we going to? Shall we drive in the car all night?" and many more such questions.

The Willing Warlock was forced to answer all these questions in the right way. If he did not answer, Jemima Jane dragged at his hair, or twisted his ear, or took hold of his nose. If the answer he gave did not please Jemima Jane, Towser rose up growling, and the Willing Warlock had quickly to think of a better answer. It was not long before he was as plastered with chocolate as Jemima Jane was. He thought that it was not possible for a person to be more unhappy.

He was wrong. Towser suddenly stood up and staggered about the backseat, making odd noises.

"Towser's going to go sick," Jemima Jane said.

The Willing Warlock squealed to a halt on the hard shoulder and threw all four doors open wide. Towser would have to get out, he thought. Then he could drive straight off again and leave Towser by the roadside.

As he thought that, Towser landed heavily on top of him. Sitting on the Willing Warlock, he got rid of the gâteau onto the edge of the motorway. It took him some time. Meanwhile the Willing Warlock wondered if Towser was actually as heavy as a cow, or whether he only felt that way.

"Now go on, go on driving," Jemima Jane said when Towser at last had finished.

The Willing Warlock obeyed. He drove on. Then it was the car's turn. It flashed a red light at him. "You are running out of petrol," it remarked.

"Good," said the Willing Warlock feelingly.

"Go on driving," said Jemima Jane, and Towser, as usual, backed her up.

The Willing Warlock drove on through the night. A new and unpleasant smell now filled the car. It did not mix well with chocolate. The Willing Warlock supposed it must be Towser. He drove and the car boringly repeated its remark about petrol until, as they passed a sign saying

BENTWELL SERVICES, the car suddenly changed its tune and said, "You have started on the reserve tank." Then it became quite talkative and added, "You have petrol for ten more miles only. You are running out of petrol—"

"I heard you," said the Willing Warlock. "I shall have to stop," he told Jemima Jane and Towser, with great relief. Then, to stop Jemima Jane telling him to drive on, and because the new smell was mixing with the chocolate worse than ever, he said, "And what is this smell in here?"

"Me," Jemima Jane said, rather defiantly. "I went in my pants. It's your fault. You didn't take me to the Ladies'."

At which Towser at once sprang up, growling, and the car added, "You are running out of petrol."

The Willing Warlock groaned aloud and went squealing into BENTWELL SERVICES. The car told him reproachfully that he was wasting petrol and then added that he was running out of it, but the Willing Warlock was too far gone to attend to it. He sprang out of the car and once more tried to run away. Towser sprang out after him and fastened his teeth in the Willing Warlock's now tattered trouser leg. And Jemima Jane scrambled out after Towser.

"Take me to the Ladies'," she said. "You have to change my pants. My clean ones are in the bag at the back."

"I can't take you to the Ladies'!" the Willing Warlock said. He had no idea what to do. What *did* one do? You have one grown-up male Warlock, one female child, and one dog fastened to the Warlock's trouser leg that might be male or female. Did you go to the Gents' or the Ladies'? The Willing Warlock just did not know.

He had to settle for doing it publicly in the car park. It made him ill. It was the last straw. Jemima Jane gave him loud directions in a ringing bossy voice. Towser growled steadily. As he struggled with the gruesome task, the Willing Warlock heard people gathering around, sniggering. He hardly cared. He was a broken Warlock by then. When he looked up to find himself in a ring of policemen and the small man in the pin-striped suit standing just beside him, he felt nothing but extreme relief. "I'll come quietly," he said.

"Hello, Daddy!" Jemima Jane shouted. She suddenly looked enchanting, in spite of the chocolate. And Towser changed character, too, and fawned and gamboled around the small man, squeaking like a puppy.

The small man picked up Jemima Jane, chocolate and all, and looked forbiddingly at the Willing Warlock. "If you've harmed Prudence, or the dog either," he said, "you're for it, you know."

"Harmed!" the Willing Warlock said hysterically. "That child's the biggest bully in the world—bar that car or that dog! And the dog's a thief, too! *I'm* the one that's harmed! Anyway, she said her name was Jemima Jane."

"That's just a jingle I taught her, to prevent people trying name magic," the small man said, laughing rather. "The dog has a secret name anyway. All Kathayack Demon Dogs do. Do you know who I am, Warlock?"

"No," said the Willing Warlock, trying not to look respectfully at the fawning Towser. He had heard of Demon Dogs. The beast probably had more magic than he did.

"Kathusa," said the man. "Financial wizard. I'm Chrestomanci's agent in this world. That crook Jean-Pierre keeps sending people here, and they all get into trouble. It's my job to pick them up. I was coming into the bank to help you, Warlock, and you go and pinch my car."

"Oh," said the Willing Warlock. The policemen coughed and began to close in. He resigned himself to a long time in prison.

But Kathusa held up a hand to stop the police-men. "See here, Warlock," he said, "you have a choice. I need a man to look after my cars and exercise Towser. You can do that and go straight, or you can go to prison. Which is it to be?"

It was a terrible choice. Towser met the Will-ing Warlock's eye and licked his lips. The Willing Warlock decided he preferred prison.

But Jemima Jane—or rather Prudence—turned to the policemen, beaming. "He's going to look after me and Towser," she announced. "He likes his nose being pulled."

The Willing Warlock tried not to groan.

STEALER OF SOULS

C AT CHANT WAS NOT altogether happy,
either with himself or with other people.
The reason was the Italian boy whom
Chrestomanci had unexpectedly brought back to
Chrestomanci Castle after his trip to Italy.

"Cat," said Chrestomanci, who was looking
rather tired after his travels, "this is Antonio
Montana. You'll find he has some very interesting
magic."

Cat looked at the Italian boy, and the Italian
boy held out his hand and said, "How do you do.
Please call me Tonino," in excellent English, but
with a slight halt at the end of each word, as if he
was used to words that mostly ended in o. Cat
knew at that instant that he was going to count
the days until someone took Tonino back to Italy
again. And he hoped someone would do it soon.

It was not just the beautiful English and the good manners. Tonino had fair hair—that almost grayish fair hair people usually call ash blond—which Cat had never imagined an Italian could have. It looked very sophisticated, and it made Cat's hair look a crude straw color by comparison. As if this was not enough, Tonino had trusting brown eyes and a nervous expression, and he was evidently younger than Cat. He looked so sweet that Cat shook hands as quickly as he could without being rude, knowing at once that everyone would expect him to look after Tonino.

"Pleased to meet you," he lied.

Sure enough, Chrestomanci said, "Cat, I'm sure I can trust you to show Tonino the ropes here and keep an eye on him until he finds his feet in England."

Cat sighed. He knew he was going to be very bored.

But it was worse than that. The other children in the castle thought Tonino was lovely. They all did their best to be friends with him. Chrestomanci's daughter, Julia, patiently taught Tonino all the games you played in England, including cricket. Chrestomanci's son, Roger, joined in the cricket lessons and then spent hours gravely comparing spells with Tonino. Chrestomanci's ward, Janet, spent further hours enthusiastically asking Tonino about Italy. Janet came from another world where Italy was quite different, and she was interested in the differences.

And yet, despite all this attention, Tonino went around with a lost, lonely look that made Cat avoid him. He could tell Tonino was acutely homesick. In fact, Cat was fairly sure Tonino was feeling just the way Cat had felt himself when he first came to Chrestomanci Castle, and Cat could not get over the annoyance of having someone have feelings that were *his*. He knew this was stupid—this was partly why he was not happy with himself—but he was not happy with Julia, Roger, and Janet either. He considered that they were making a stupid fuss over Tonino. The fact was that Julia and Roger normally looked after Cat. He had grown used to being the youngest and unhappiest person in the castle until Tonino had come along and stolen his thunder. Cat knew all this perfectly well, but it did not make the slightest difference to the way he felt.

To make things worse, Chrestomanci himself was extremely interested in Tonino's magic. He spent large parts of the next few days with Tonino doing experiments to discover just what the extent of Tonino's powers was, while Cat, who was used to being the one with the interesting magic, was left to wrestle with problems of magic theory by himself in Chrestomanci's study.

"Tonino," Chrestomanci said, by way of explanation, "can, it seems, not only reinforce other people's spells but also make use of any magic other people do. If it's true, it's a highly unusual ability. And by the way," he added, turning around in the doorway, looking tall enough to brush the ceiling, "you don't seem to have shown Tonino around the castle yet. How come?"

"I was busy—I forgot," Cat muttered sulkily.

"Fit it into your crowded schedule soon, please," Chrestomanci said, "or I may find myself becoming seriously irritated."

Cat sighed but nodded. No one disobeyed Chrestomanci when he got like this. But now he had to face the fact that Chrestomanci knew exactly how Cat was feeling and had absolutely no patience with it. Cat sighed again as he got down to his problems.

Magic Theory left him completely bewildered. His trouble was that he could, instinctively, do magic that used very advanced Magic Theory indeed, and he had no idea how he did it. Sometimes he did not even know he was doing magic. Chrestomanci said Cat *must* learn theory or he might one day do something quite terrible by mistake. As far as Cat was concerned, the one thing he wanted magic to do was to solve theory problems, and that seemed to be the one thing you couldn't use it for.

He got six answers he knew were nonsense. Then, feeling very neglected and put-upon, he took Tonino on a tour of the castle. It was not a success. Tonino looked white and tired and timid almost the whole time and shivered in the long, cold passages and on all the dark, chilly staircases. Cat could not think of anything to say except utterly obvious things like "This is called the small drawing room" or "This is the schoolroom, we have lessons here with Michael Saunders, but he's away in Greenland just now" or "Here's the front hall, it's made of marble."

The only time Tonino showed the slightest interest was when they came to the big windows that overlooked the velvety green lawn and the great cedars of the gardens. He actually hooked a knee on the windowsill to look down at it.

"My mother has told me of this," he said, "but

I never thought it would be so wet and green."

"How does your mother know about the gardens?" Cat asked.

"She is English. She was brought up here in this castle when Gabriel de Witt, who was Chrestomanci before this one, collected many children with magic talents to be trained here," Tonino replied.

Cat felt annoyed and somehow cheated that Tonino had a connection with the castle anyway. "Then you're English, too," he said. It came out as if he were accusing Tonino of a crime.

"No, I am Italian," Tonino said firmly. He added, with great pride, "I belong to the foremost spell house in Italy."

There did not seem to be any reply to this. Cat did think of saying, "And I'm going to be the next Chrestomanci—I've got nine lives, you know," but he knew this would be silly and boastful. Tonino had not been boasting really. He had been trying to say why he did not belong in the castle. So Cat simply took Tonino back to the playroom, where Julia was only too ready to teach him card games, and mooched away, feeling he had done his duty. He tried to avoid Tonino after that. He did not like being made to feel the way Tonino made him feel.

Unfortunately, Julia went down with measles the next day, and Roger the day after that. Cat had had measles long before he came to the castle, and so had Tonino. Janet could not remember whether she had had them or not, although she assured them that there was measles in the world she came from, because you could be injected against it. "Maybe I've been injected," she suggested hopefully.

Chrestomanci's wife, Millie, gave Janet a worried look. "I think you'd better stay away from Roger and Julia all the same," she said.

"But you're an enchantress," Janet said. "You could stop me getting them."

"Magic has almost no effect on measles," Millie told her. "I wish it did, but it doesn't. Cat can see Roger and Julia if he wants, but you keep away."

Cat went to Roger's bedroom and then Julia's and was shocked at how ill they both were. He could see it was going to be weeks before they were well enough to look after Tonino. He found himself, quite urgently and cold-bloodedly (and in spite of what Millie had said) putting a spell on Janet to make sure she did not go down with measles, too. He knew as he did it that it was probably the most selfish thing he had ever done, but he simply could not bear to be the only one left to look after Tonino. By the time he got back to the schoolroom, he was in a very bad mood.

"How are they?" Janet asked him anxiously.

"Awful," Cat said out of his bad mood. "Roger's sort of purple and Julia's uglier than ever."

"Do you think Julia's ugly then?" Janet said. "I mean, in the normal way."

"Yes," said Cat. "Plump and pudgy, like you said."

"I was angry when I told you that and being unfair," said Janet. "You shouldn't believe me when I'm angry, Cat. I'll take a bet with you, if you like, that Julia grows up a raving beauty, as good-looking as her father. She's got his bones to her face. And, you must admit, Chrestomanci is taller and darker and handsomer than any man has any right to be!"

She kept giving little dry coughs as she spoke. Cat examined her with concern. Janet's extremely pretty face showed no sign of any spots, but her golden hair was hanging in lifeless hanks, and her big blue eyes were slightly red about the rims. He suspected that he had been too late with his spell.

"And Roger?" he asked. "Is he going to grow up ravingly beautiful, too?"

Janet looked dubious. "He takes after Millie. But," she added, coughing again, "he'll be very nice."

"Not like me then," Cat said sadly. "I'm nastier than everyone. I think I'm growing into an evil enchanter. And I think you've got measles, too."

"I have *not!*" Janet exclaimed indignantly.

But she had. By that evening she was in bed, too, freckled purple all over and looking uglier than Julia. The maids once again ran up and down stairs with possets to bring down fever, while Millie used the new telephone at the top of the marble stairs to ask the doctor to call again.

"I shall go mad," she told Cat. "Janet's really ill, worse than the other two. Go and make sure Tonino's not feeling too neglected, there's a good boy."

I knew it! Cat thought, and went very slowly back to the playroom.

Behind him the telephone rang again. He heard Millie answer it. He had gone three slow steps when he heard the telephone go back on its rest. Millie uttered a great groan, and Chrestomanci at once came out of the office to see what was wrong. Cat prudently made himself invisible.

"Oh, lord!" Millie said. "That was Mordecai Roberts. Why does everything happen at once? Gabriel de Witt wants to see Tonino tomorrow."

"That's awkward," Chrestomanci said. "Tomorrow I've *got* to be in Series One for the Conclave of Mages."

"But I really *must* stay here with the other children," Millie said. "Janet's going to need all magic can do for her, particularly for her eyes. Can we put Gabriel off?"

"I don't think so," Chrestomanci replied, unusually seriously. "Tomorrow could be Gabriel's last chance to see anyone. His lives are leaving him steadily now. And he was thrilled when I told him about Tonino. He's always hoped we'd find someone with backup magic one day. I know what, though. We can send Cat with Tonino. Gabriel's almost equally interested in Cat, and the responsibility will do Cat good."

No, it won't! Cat thought. I *hate* responsibility! As he fled invisibly back to the playroom, he thought, Why *me*? Why can't they send one of the wizards on the staff, or Miss Bessemer, or someone? But of course everyone was going to be busy, with Chrestomanci away and Millie looking after Janet.

In the playroom Tonino was curled up on one of the shabby sofas deep in one of Julia's favorite books. He barely looked up as the door seemed to open by itself and Cat shook himself visible again.

Tonino, Cat realized, was an avid reader. He knew the signs from Janet and Julia. That was a relief. Cat went quietly away to his own room and collected all the books there that Janet had been trying to make him read and that Cat had somehow not got around to—how could Janet expect him to read books called *Millie Goes to School* anyway?—and brought the whole armful back to the playroom.

"Here," he said, dumping them on the floor beside Tonino. "Janet says these are good."

And he thought, as he curled up on the other battered sofa, that this was exactly how a person got to be an evil enchanter, by doing a whole lot of good things for bad reasons. He tried to think of ways to get out of looking after Tonino tomorrow.

Cat always dreaded going to visit Gabriel de Witt anyway. He was so old-fashioned and sharp and so obviously an enchanter, and you had to remember to behave in an old-fashioned polite way all the time you were there. But these days it was worse than that. As Chrestomanci had said, old Gabriel's nine lives were leaving him one by one. Every time Cat was taken to see him, Gabriel de Witt looked iller and older and more gaunt, and Cat's secret dread was that one day he would be there, making polite conversation, and actually *see* one of Gabriel's lives as it went away. If he did, he knew he would scream.

The dread of this happening so haunted Cat that he could scarcely speak to Gabriel for watching and waiting for a life to leave. Gabriel de Witt told Chrestomanci that Cat was a strange, reserved boy. To which Chrestomanci answered "Really?" in his most sarcastic way.

People, Cat thought, should be looking after *him*, and not breaking his spirit by forcing him to take Italian boys to see elderly enchanters. But he could think of no way to get out of it that Millie or Chrestomanci would not see through at once. Chrestomanci seemed to know when Cat was being dishonest even before Cat knew it himself. Cat sighed and went to bed hoping that Chrestomanci would have changed his mind in the morning and decided to send someone else with Tonino.

This was not to be. At breakfast Chrestomanci appeared (in a sea green dressing gown with a design of waves breaking on it) to tell Cat and Tonino that they were catching the ten-thirty train to Dulwich to visit Gabriel de Witt. Then he went away, and Millie, who looked very tired from having sat up half the night with Janet, rustled in to give them their train fare.

Tonino frowned. "I do not understand. Was not Monsignor de Witt the former Chrestomanci, Lady Chant?"

"Call me Millie, please," said Millie. "Yes, that's right. Gabriel stayed in the post until he felt Christopher was ready to take over, and then he retired— Oh, I *see*! You thought he was *dead*! Oh, no, far from it. Gabriel's as lively and sharp as ever he was, you'll see."

There was a time when Cat had thought that the last Chrestomanci was dead, too. He had thought that the present Chrestomanci had to die before the next one took over, and he used to watch this Chrestomanci rather anxiously in case Chrestomanci showed signs of losing his last two lives and thrusting Cat into all the huge responsibility of looking after the magic in this world. He had been quite relieved to find it was more normal than that.

"There's nothing to worry about," Millie said. "Mordecai Roberts is going to meet you at the station, and then he'll take you back there in a cab after lunch. And Tom is going to drive you to the station here in the car and meet you off the three-nineteen when you get back. Here's the money, Cat, and an extra five shillings in case you need a snack on the way back—because efficient as I *know* Miss Rosalie is, she doesn't have any idea how much boys need to eat. She never did have, and she hasn't changed. And I want to hear all about it when you get home."

She gave them a warm hug each and rushed away, murmuring, "Lemon barley, febrifuge in half an hour, and then the eye salve."

Tonino pushed away his cocoa. "I think I am ill on trains."

This proved to be true. Luckily Cat managed to get them a carriage to themselves after the young man who acted as Chrestomanci's secretary had dropped them at the station. Tonino sat at the far corner of the smoky little space, with the window pulled down as low as it would go and his handkerchief pressed to his mouth. Though he did not actually bring up his breakfast, he went whiter and whiter, until Cat could hardly credit that a person could be so pale.

"Were you like this all the way from Italy?" Cat asked him, slightly awed.

"Rather worse," Tonino said through the handkerchief, and swallowed desperately.

Cat knew he should sympathize. He got travel-sick himself, but only in cars. But instead of feeling sorry for Tonino, he did not know whether to feel superior or annoyed that Tonino, once again, was more to be pitied than *he* was.

At least it meant that Cat did not have to talk to him.

Dulwich was a pleasant village a little south of London and, once the train had chuffed away from the platform, full of fresh air swaying the trees. Tonino breathed the air deeply and began to get his color back.

"Bad traveler, is he?" Mordecai Roberts asked sympathetically as he led them to the cab waiting for them outside the station.

This Mr. Mordecai Roberts always puzzled Cat slightly. With his light, almost white, curly hair and his dark coffee complexion, he looked a great deal more foreign than Tonino did, and yet when he spoke, it was in perfect, unforeign English. It was educated English, too, which was another puzzle, because Cat had always vaguely supposed that Mr. Roberts was a sort of valet hired to look after Gabriel de Witt in his retirement. But Mr. Roberts also seemed to be a strong magic user. He looked at Cat rather reproachfully as they got into the cab and said, "There are hundreds of spells against travel sickness, you know."

"I think I did stop him being sick," Cat said uncomfortably. Here was his old problem again, of not being sure when he was using magic and when he was not. But what really made Cat uncomfortable was the knowledge that if he *had* used magic on Tonino, it was not for Tonino's sake. Cat hated seeing people be sick. Here he was doing a good thing for a bad selfish reason again. At this rate he was, quite definitely, going to end up as an evil enchanter.

Gabriel de Witt lived in a spacious, comfortable modern house with wide windows and a metal rail along the roof in the latest style. It was set among trees on a new road that gave the house a view of the countryside beyond.

Miss Rosalie threw open its clean white front

door and welcomed them all inside. She was a funny little woman with a lot of gray in her black hair, who always, invariably, wore gray lace mittens. She was another puzzle. There was a big gold wedding ring lurking under the gray lace of her left-hand mitten, which Cat *thought* might mean she was married to Mr. Roberts, but she always had to be called Miss Rosalie. For another thing, she behaved as if she were a witch. But she wasn't. As she shut the front door, she made brisk gestures as if she were setting wards of safety on it. But it was Mr. Roberts who really set the wards.

"You'll have to go upstairs, boys," Miss Rosalie said. "I kept him in bed today. He was fretting himself ill about meeting young Antonio. So excited about the new magic. Up this way."

They followed Miss Rosalie up the deeply carpeted stairs and into a big sunny bedroom, where white curtains were gently blowing at the big windows. Everything possible was white—the walls, the carpet, the bed with its stacked white pillows and white bedspread, the spray of lilies of the valley on the bedside table—and so neat that it looked like a room no one was using.

"Ah, Eric Chant and Antonio Montana!" Gabriel de Witt said from the bank of pillows.

His thin, dry voice sounded quite eager. "Glad to see you. Come and take a seat where I can look at you."

Two plain white chairs had been set one on each side of the bed and about halfway down it. Tonino slid sideways into the nearest, looking thoroughly intimidated. Cat could understand that. He thought, as he went around to the other chair, that the whiteness of the room must be to make Gabriel de Witt show up. Gabriel was so thin and pale that you would hardly have seen him among ordinary colors. His white hair melted into the white of the pillows. His face had shrunk so that it seemed like two caves, made from Gabriel's jutting cheekbones and his tall white forehead, out of which two strong eyes glared feverishly. Cat tried not to look at the tangle of white chest hair sticking out of the white nightshirt under Gabriel's too-pointed chin. It seemed indecent, somehow.

But probably the most upsetting thing, Cat thought as he sat down, was the smell of illness and old man in the room and the way that, in spite of the whiteness, there was a darkness at the edges of everything. The corners of the room felt gray, and they loomed. Cat kept his eyes on Gabriel's long, veiny enchanter's hands, folded together on the white bedspread, because these seemed the most normal things about him, and hoped this visit would not last too long.

"Now, young Antonio," Gabriel said, and his pale lips moved in a dry way Cat could not look at, "I hear that your best magic is done when you use someone else's spell."

Tonino nodded timidly. "I think so, sir."

Cat kept his eyes on Gabriel's unmoving, folded hands and braced himself for an hour or more of talk about magic theory. But to his surprise, the kind of talk Cat could not understand only went on for about five minutes. Then Gabriel was saying, "In that case I would like to try a little experiment, with your permission. A very little simple one. As you can see, I am very feeble today. I would like to do a small enchantment to enable myself to sit up, but I believe it would not come to much without your help. Would you do that for me?"

"Of course," Tonino said. "Would—would a strength spell be correct for this? I would have to sing, if that is all right, because that is the way we do things in the Casa Montana."

"By all means," agreed Gabriel. "When you're ready then."

Tonino put back his head and sang, to Cat's surprise, very sweetly and tunefully, in what seemed to be Latin, while Gabriel's hands moved on the bedspread, just slightly. As the song finished, the pillows behind Gabriel's head rebuilt themselves into a swelling stack, which pushed the old man into sitting position. After that, they pushed him away from themselves so that he was sitting up on his own, quite steadily.

"Well done!" said Gabriel. He was clearly delighted. A faint pink crept over his jutting cheeks, and his eyes glittered in their caves. "You have very strong and unusual magic, young man." He turned eagerly to Cat. "Now I can talk to you, Eric. This is important. Are your remaining lives quite safe? I have reason to believe that someone is looking for them as well as for mine."

Cat's mind went to a certain cardboard book of matches, more than half of them used. "Well, Chrestomanci has them locked in the castle safe, with a lot of spells on them. They feel all right."

Gabriel's eyes glittered into distance while he considered Cat's lives, too. "True," he said. "They feel secure. But I was never totally happy while Christopher's other life was locked in there. I put his last life into a gold ring, you know, and locked it in that same safe—this was at a time when he seemed to be losing a life once a week, and something had to be done, you understand—but it was a great relief to me when he married and we could give the life to Millie as her wedding ring. I would greatly prefer it if your lives were equally well guarded. A book of matches is such a flimsy thing."

Cat knew this. But Chrestomanci seemed to him to be the best guardian there could be. "Who do you think is looking for them?" he asked.

"Now that is the odd thing," Gabriel answered, still looking into distance. "The only person who seems to fit the shapes of the magics I am sensing has, I swear, been dead and gone at least two hundred years. An enchanter known as Neville Spiderman. He was one of the last of the really bad ones."

Cat stared at Gabriel staring into distance like a bony old prophet. On the other side of the bed, Tonino was staring, too, looking as scared as Cat felt. "What," Cat asked huskily, "makes you think it might be someone from the past?"

"For this reason—" Gabriel began.

Then the thing Cat had been dreading happened.

Gabriel de Witt's face suddenly lost all expression. Behind him, the pillows began slowly subsiding, letting the old man down into lying position again. As they did so, Gabriel de Witt seemed to climb out of himself. A tall old man in a long white nightshirt unfolded himself from the old man who was lying down and stood for a moment looking rather sadly from Cat to Tonino, before he walked away into a distance that was somehow not part of the white bedroom.

Both their heads turned to follow him as he walked. Cat realized he could see Tonino through the shape of the departing old man, and the lilies of the valley on the bedside table, and then the corner of the white wardrobe. The old man was getting smaller all the time as he walked, until at last he was lost into white distance.

Cat was astonished not to find himself screaming—although he almost did when he looked back at Gabriel de Witt lying on his pillows and found Gabriel's face blue-pale and more sunken than ever, and his mouth slowly dropping wider and wider open. Cat could not seem to utter a sound, or move either, until Tonino whispered, "I saw you *through* him!"

Cat gulped. "Me, too. I saw you. Why was that?"

"Was that his last life?" Tonino asked. "Is he truly dead now?"

"I don't know," said Cat. "I think we ought to call someone."

But it seemed as if someone already knew. Footsteps thumped on the carpet outside and Miss Rosalie burst into the room, followed by Mr. Roberts. They both rushed to the bed and stared anxiously down at Gabriel de Witt as if they expected him to wake up any minute. Cat snatched another look at that gaping mouth and strange blue-wax complexion, and thought that he had never seen anyone more obviously dead. He had seen his parents just before their funeral, but they had looked almost asleep and not like this at all.

"Don't worry, boys," Miss Rosalie said. "It's only another life gone. He's still got two more."

"No, you're forgetting the life he gave to Asheth," Mr. Roberts reminded her.

"Oh, so I am," Miss Rosalie said. "Silly of me. But he's still got one left. Why don't you go downstairs, boys, until the new life takes over? It can sometimes be quite a while."

Cat and Tonino jumped thankfully out of their chairs. But as they did so, Gabriel stirred.

His mouth shut with a snap and his face became the face of a person again—a person who looked pale and unwell, but full of strong feelings despite that.

"Rosalie," he said, weak and fretful, "warn Chrestomanci. Neville Spiderman is sniffing around this house. I felt him very clearly just now."

"Oh, nonsense, Gabriel!" Miss Rosalie said, brisk and bossy. "How *could* he be? You *know* Neville Spiderman—whatever his real name was—lived at the time of the first Chrestomanci. That was more than a hundred years before you were born!"

"I felt him, I tell you!" Gabriel insisted. "He was there when my last life was leaving."

"You can't possibly know that," Miss Rosalie insisted.

"I do know. I made a study of the man," Gabriel insisted in return. His voice was more and more weak and quavery. "When I was first made Chrestomanci, I *studied* him, because I needed to know what a really evil enchanter was like and he was the most ingenious of the lot. And this is very ingenious, Rosalie. He's trying to make himself stronger than any Chrestomanci ever was. Warn Christopher he's not safe. Warn Eric particularly."

"Yes, yes, yes," Miss Rosalie said, so obviously humoring him that Gabriel began rolling about in distress, spilling bedclothes on to the floor. "Of course I'll warn them," Miss Rosalie said, hauling blankets back. "Settle down, Gabriel, before you make yourself ill, and we'll do everything you want." She made meaningful faces at Mr. Roberts to take Cat and Tonino out of the room.

Mr. Roberts nodded. He put a hand on each boy's shoulder and steered them out onto the landing. Behind them, as he gently shut the door, they heard Gabriel say, "Listen, Rosalie, my mind is *not* wandering! Spiderman has learned to travel in time. He's dangerous. I mean what I say."

Gabriel de Witt sounded so weak and so upset that Mr. Roberts said, looking extremely worried, "Look, I think you boys had better go home now. I don't think he'll be well enough to talk to you again today. I'll call you a cab and telephone the castle to say you'll be back on an earlier train."

There was nothing Cat wanted more by this time. Tonino, from the look of him, felt the same. The only thing Cat regretted was that they were going to miss lunch. Still, Miss Rosalie's idea of lunch was usually a tomato and some lettuce, and they did have Millie's five shillings. He followed

Mr. Roberts downstairs, thinking of doughnuts and station pies.

Luckily there was a cab just clopping along the road as they reached the front gate. It was one of those old-fashioned horse-drawn hackneys, like a big upright box on wheels, with the driver sitting up on top of the box. It was shabby and the horse was scrawny, but Mr. Roberts hailed it with strong relief and paid the driver for them as the boys climbed in. "You can just catch the twelve-thirty," he said. "Hurry it along, driver."

He shut the door and the cab set off. It was smelly and jolting, and its wheels squeaked, but Cat felt it was worth it just to get away so soon. It was not far to the station. Cat sat back in the half dark inside the box and felt his mind go empty with relief. He did not want to think of Gabriel de Witt again for a very long time. He thought about station pies and corned beef sandwiches instead.

But half an hour of jolting, smelling, and squeaking later, something began puzzling him. He turned to the other boy in the dimness beside him. "Where were we going?"

Tonino—if that was his name; Cat found he was not at all sure—shook his head uncertainly.

"We are traveling northeast," he said. "I feel sick."

"Keep swallowing then," Cat told him. One thing he seemed to be sure of was that he was supposed to look after this boy, whoever he was. "It can't be that far now," he said soothingly. Then he wondered what, or where, was "not far." He was a little puzzled to find he had no idea.

At least he seemed to be right about its not being far. Five minutes later, just as the other boy's swallowing was getting quite desperate, the cab squealed to a stop with a great yell of "Whoa there!" from the driver up above, and the door beside Cat was pulled open. Cat blinked out into gray light upon a dirty pavement and a row of old, old houses as far as he could see in both directions. We must be in the outskirts of London, he thought. While Cat puzzled about this, the driver said, "Two blondie lads, just like you said, governor."

The person who had opened the door leaned around it to peer in at them. They found themselves face-to-face with a smallish elderly man in a dirty black gown. The peering round brown eyes and the brown whiskery face, full of lines and wrinkles, were so like a monkey's that it was only the soft black priestly sort of hat on the man's head that showed he was a man and not a monkey. Or probably not. Cat found, in some strange way, that he was not sure of anything.

The monkey's flat mouth spread in a grin. "Ah, yes, the right two," the man said, "as ordered." He had a dry, snapping voice, which snapped out, "Out you get then. Make haste now."

While Cat and Tonino obediently scrambled out to find themselves in a long street of the old tumbledown houses—all slightly different, like cottages built for a town—the man in the black gown handed up a gold coin to the driver. "Charmed to take you back," he muttered. It was hard to tell if he was speaking to himself or to the driver, but the driver touched his hat to him anyway with great respect, cracked his whip, and drove away, squealing and clattering. The cab seemed to move away from them up the tumbledown street in jerks, and each jerk seemed to make it harder to see. Before it quite reached the end of the street, it had jerked out of sight entirely.

They stared after it. "Why did that happen?" Tonino asked.

"Belongs to the future, doesn't it?" the monkeylike man snapped. Again he might have been talking to himself. But he seemed to notice them then. "Come along now. No stupid questions. It's not every day I hire two apprentices from the poorhouse, and I want you indoors earning your keep. Come along."

He turned and hurried into the house beside them. They followed, quite bewildered, past an unpainted front door—which closed with a slam behind them—into a dark, wooden hallway. Beyond this was a big room that was much lighter because of a row of filthy windows looking out onto bushes. As the monkey-man hurried them on through it, Cat recognized the place as a magician's workshop. It breathed out the smell of magic and of dragon's blood, and there were symbols chalked over most of the floor. Cat had a tantalizing feeling that he should have known what most of those symbols were supposed to do, and that they were not quite in any order he was used to, but when he thought about this, the symbols meant nothing to him.

The main thing he noticed was the row of star charts along one wall. There were eight of them, getting newer and newer from the old, brown one at the far left, to the one on the right, after a gap where a ninth chart had been torn down, which was white and freshly drawn.

"Gave up on that one. Too well protected," the monkey-man remarked as Cat looked at the gap. Again he was probably talking to himself, for he swung around at once and opened a door at the end of the room. "Come along, come along," he snapped, and hurried on down a sideways flight of stone steps into the cold stone basement under the house. Cat, as he hurried after, only had time to think that the last chart, after the torn-down one, had looked uncomfortably familiar in some way, before the monkey-man swung around on both of them at the bottom of the steps. "Now then," he said, "what are your names?"

It seemed a perfectly reasonable thing to ask, but they stood shivering on the chilly flagstones, staring from him to one another. Neither of them had the least idea.

The man sighed at their stupidity. "Too much of the forgettery," he muttered in that way that seemed to be talking to himself. He pointed to Cat. "All right," he said to Tonino. "What's *his* name?"

"Er—" said Tonino, "it means something. In Latin, I think. Felix, or something like that. Yes, Felix."

"And," the man said to Cat, "*his* name is?"

"Tony," said Cat. This did not strike him as quite right, any more than Felix did, but he did not seem to be able to get any closer than that. "His name's Tony."

"Not Eric?" snapped the man. "Which of you is Eric?"

They both shook their heads, although Cat had a faint, fleeting idea that the name meant a protected kind of heather. That was such an idiotic idea that he gave it up at once.

"Very well," snapped the man. "Tony and Felix, you are now my apprentices. This room here is where you will eat and sleep. You will find mattresses over there." He pointed a brown, hairy hand at a dim corner. "In that other corner there are brooms and dustpan. I require you to sweep this room and make it as clean and tidy as you can. When that is done, you may lay out the mattresses."

"Please, sir—" Tonino began. He stopped, looking frightened, as the withered old monkey face swung around to stare at him. Then he said something that was obviously not what he had started to say. "Please, sir, what should we call you?"

"I am known as Master Spiderman," snapped

the man. "You will address me as Master."

Cat felt a small, chilly jolt of alarm at the name. He put it down to the fact that he was already disliking this monkey-faced old man very much indeed. There was a smell that came off him, of old clothes, mustiness, and illness, which reminded Cat of—of—of something he could not quite remember, except that it made him frightened and uneasy. So, to make himself feel better, he said what he knew Tonino had really been going to say.

"Sir, we haven't had any lunch yet."

Master Spiderman's round monkey eyes blinked Cat's way. "Is that so? Well, you may have food as soon as you have swept and tidied this room." At that, he turned and ran up the stone steps to the door, with his musty black coat swirling. He stopped at the top. "Do not try to do any magic," he said. "I'll have nothing like that here. Nothing stupid. This place is in a time apart from any other time, and you must behave yourselves here." He went out through the door and shut it behind him. They heard a bolt shoot home on the other side of it.

That door was the only way out of the basement. The only other opening in the stone walls was a high-up window, fast shut and too dirty to see through, which let in a meager gray light. Cat and Tonino stared from the door to the window, and then at one another. "What did he mean," asked Tonino, "to do no magic? Can you do magic?"

"I don't *think* so," said Cat. "Can you?"

"I—I can't remember," Tonino said miserably. "I am blank."

So was Cat, whenever he thought about it. He was uncertain of everything, including why they were here and whether he ought to be frightened about it or just miserable. He clung to the two things he was certain about: Tonino was younger than he was, and Cat ought to be looking after him.

Tonino was shivering. "Let's find the brooms and start sweeping," Cat said. "It'll warm us up, and he'll give us something to eat when we've done it."

"He *might*," Tonino said. "Do you believe him or trust him?"

"No," said Cat. This was something else his fuzzy mind was clear about completely. "We'd better not give him an excuse not to give us any food."

They found two worn-down brooms and a long-handled dustpan in the corner by the stairs, along with a heap of amazingly various rubbish—rusty cans, cobwebby planks, rags so old they had turned into piles of dirt, walking sticks, broken jars, butterfly nets, fishing rods, half a carriage wheel, broken umbrellas, works of clocks, and things that had decayed too much for anyone to guess what they had once been—and they set about cleaning the room.

Without needing to discuss it, they started at the end where the stairs were. It was clearer that end. The rest of the room was filled with a clutter of old splintery workbenches and broken chairs, which got more and more jumbled toward the far end, where the entire wall was completely draped in cobwebs, thicker and dustier than Cat would have thought possible. For another thing, when they were near the stairs, they could hear Master Spiderman creaking and muttering about in the room overhead, and it seemed reasonable to think that he could hear them, too. It was in both their minds that if he heard them truly hard at work, he might decide to bring them something to eat.

They swept for what seemed hours. They used the least smelly of the old rags for dusters. Cat found an old sack, into which they noisily poured panloads of dust, cobwebs, and broken glass. They thumped with their brooms. Tonino hauled out another load of rubbish from another corner, making a tremendous clatter, and found the mattresses among it. They were filthy, lumpy things, so damp they felt wet.

Cat slammed about making a heap of the most broken chairs and hung the mattresses over it in a gust of mildew smell, to air. By this time, slightly to Cat's surprise, more than half the room was clear. Dust hung in the air, making Tonino's nose and eyes run, filling their clothes and their hair, and streaking their faces with gray. Their hands were black, and their fingernails blacker. They were hungry, thirsty, and tired out.

"I need a drink," Tonino croaked.

Cat swept the stairs a second time, very noisily, but Master Spiderman gave no sign of having heard. Perhaps if he called out . . . ? It seemed to take a real effort to muster the courage. And, somehow, Cat could not bring himself to call Master Spiderman Master, try as he would. He knocked politely on the door and called out, "Excuse me, sir! Excuse me, please, we're terribly thirsty."

There was no reply. When Cat put his ear to

the door, he could no longer hear any sounds of Master Spiderman moving about. He came gloomily back down the stairs. "I don't think he's there now."

Tonino sighed. "He will know when this room is cleared and he will come back then, but not before. I am fairly sure he is an enchanter."

"There's nothing to stop us having a rest anyway," Cat said. He dragged the two mattresses over to the wall and made a seat out of them. They both sat down thankfully. The mattresses were still extremely damp and they smelled horrible. Both of them tried not to notice. "How do you know he's an enchanter?" Cat asked, to take his mind off the smell and the wetness.

"The eyes," said Tonino. "Your eyes are the same."

Cat thought of Master Spiderman's round, glossy eyes and shuddered. "They're nothing *like* the same!" he said. "My eyes are blue."

Tonino put his head down and held it in both hands. "Sorry," he said. "For a moment I thought you were an enchanter. Now I don't know what I think."

This made Cat shift about uncomfortably. It was frightening, if he let himself notice it, how whenever he thought about anything, particularly about magic, there seemed to be nothing to think. There seemed to be only here and now in this cold basement, and the horrible bad-breath smell coming up from the mattresses, and the damp creeping up with the smell and coming through his clothes.

Beside him, Tonino was shivering again. "This is no good," Cat said. "Get up."

Tonino climbed to his feet. "I think it is a spell to keep us obedient," he said. "He told us we could lay the mattresses out *after* the room was clean."

"I don't care," said Cat. He picked up the top mattress and shook it, trying to shake the smell— or the spell—out.

This proved to be a bad mistake. The whole basement became full, almost instantly, of thick, choking, bad-smelling, chaffy dust. They could hardly see one another. What Cat could see of Tonino was alarming. He was bending over, coughing and coughing, a terrible hacking cough, with a whooping, choking sound whenever Tonino tried to breathe in. It sounded as if Tonino were choking to death, and it frightened Cat out of what few wits he seemed to have.

He dropped the mattress in a further cloud of dust, snatched up a broom, and in a frenzy of fear and guilt ran up the stairs, where he battered on the door with the broom handle. "Help!" he screamed. "Tony's suffocating! *Help!*"

Nothing happened. As soon as Cat stopped beating on the door, he could tell from the sort of silence beyond that Master Spiderman was not bothering to listen. He ran down again, into the thick, thick dust, seized the choking Tonino by one elbow, and pushed him up the stairs.

"Get up by the door," he said. "It's clearer there." He could hear Tonino choking his way upward as he himself ran toward the dirty, murky high-up window and slammed the end of the broom handle into it like a spear.

Cat had meant to smash out a pane. But the grimy glass simply splintered into a white star and would not break any further however hard Cat poked at it with the broom. By this time he was coughing almost as wretchedly as Tonino. And angry. Master Spiderman was trying to break their spirits. Well, he was not going to! Cat dragged one of the heavy, splintery workbenches under the window and climbed on it.

The window was one of the kind that slides

up and down. Standing on the bench brought Cat's nose level with the rusty old catch that held the two halves shut in the middle. He took hold of the catch and wrenched at it angrily. It came to pieces in his hand, but at least it was not holding the window shut anymore. Cat threw the broken pieces down and gripped the dirty frame with both sets of fingers. And pulled. And heaved. And rattled.

"Let me help," Tonino said hoarsely, climbing up beside Cat, and breathed out hugely because he had been holding his breath as he came across the room.

Cat moved to one side gratefully and they both pulled. To their joy, the top half of the window juddered and slid, making an opening about four inches wide above their heads. Through it, they could just see the bottom of a set of railings, level with the pavement outside, and pairs of feet walking past—feet in old-fashioned sorts of shoes with high heels and buckles on the front.

This struck them as strange. So did the way that warm wafts of fresh air came blowing in their faces through the open gap at the same time as clouds of the dust went streaming out. But they did not stop to think about either of these things. It had dawned on both of them that if they could pull the top half of the window right down, they could climb through and get away. They hung by their hands from the top of the window, pulling grimly.

But no amount of pulling seemed to get the window any further open. As Cat left off, panting, Tonino hammered the lower half of the window with his fist and shouted at the next pair of buckled shoes that walked past.

"Help! Help! We're shut in!"

The feet went by without pausing.

"They didn't hear," said Cat. "It must be a spell."

"Then what do we *do*?" Tonino wailed. "I am so hungry!"

So was Cat. As far as he could tell, it was at least teatime by then. He thought of tea going on at the castle, with cress sandwiches and cream cakes— Hang on! *What* castle? But the flash of memory was gone, leaving just the notion of cress sandwiches, luxurious ones with all the crusts cut off, and cakes oozing jam and cream. Cat's stomach grumbled, and he felt ready to wail like Tonino. But he knew he had to be sensible, because he was older than Tonino.

"He said we could have food when we'd cleaned the whole room," he reminded Tonino. "We'd better get on and finish it."

They climbed down and set to work again. This time Cat tried to organize it properly. He made sure they worked only in short bursts, and he found two not-so-broken chairs so that they could sit on them and rest while the latest lot of dust was sucked away out through the open window. Slowly they worked their way toward the far end of the basement. By the time the light filtering in past the dirt on the window was golden, late-evening light, they were ready to start on the end wall.

They were not looking forward to this. From ceiling to floor, that end was draped in a mass of filthy, dust-hung cobwebs at least two feet thick, fluttering and heaving gray and sinister in the small draft from the window. Under the draped webs, they could just see another of the splintery workbenches. On it, in the very middle, there seemed to be a small black container of some kind.

"What do you think that is?" Tonino wondered.

"I'll see. More old rubbish, I expect." Cat

shudderingly put his left hand through the cob-webs, hating the sticky, tender touch of them, and took hold of the black thing.

As soon as his fingers closed around it, he had a feeling it was important. But when he had pulled it gently out, avoiding touching the cobwebs where he could, it was just an old black canister with a round hole clumsily punched in its lid. "Only a tin tea caddy," he said. "It looks as if someone's tried to make it into a money box." He shook it. Something inside rattled quite sharply.

"See what's in there," said Tonino. "It might be valuable."

Cat pried at the lid, getting a big new patch of black dirt on his front as he did so. The tin was coated in generations of sooty grease. But the lid was quite easy to move and came off with a clat-ter. Inside were a very few red kidney beans. Seven of them.

Cat tipped them out onto his hand to be sure, and they were indeed, most disappointingly, beans. They must have been in that tin a very long time. Four of them were wrinkled and shriveled, and one was so old it was just a withered brown lump. It was clear they were nothing valuable at all.

"Beans!" Cat said disgustedly.

"Oh, yes," said Tonino, "but think of Jack and the Beanstalk."

They stared at one another. In an enchanter's basement anything was possible. Both had visions of mighty bean plants growing through the ceiling and on through the roof of the house, and each of them climbing one, away from Master Spiderman and out of his power. And while they stared, they heard the sound of the door being unbolted at the other end of the room.

Cat hastily thrust the handful of beans into his pocket and jammed the lid back on the canister while Tonino picked up his broom. Tonino waited until Cat had carefully put the old tin back through the cobwebs, into the dust-free circle on the wooden bench where it had stood before, and then reached up with the broom and began virtuously sweeping billows of cobweb off the wall.

Master Spiderman threw open the door and raced down the stone steps, shouting, "No, no, no, you wretched boy! Stop that at once! Don't you know a spell when you see one?" He came rushing through the room and advanced on Tonino with his hand raised in a fist.

Tonino dropped the broom with a clatter and backed away. Cat was not sure whether Master

Spiderman was going to hit Tonino or cast a spell on him, but he got between them quickly anyway. "You've no call to hurt him," he said. "You told us to clean the place up."

For a moment, Master Spiderman bent over the two of them, clearly seething with rage. Cat smelled the unclean old-man smell from Master Spiderman's breath and the mildew from his black coat. He looked into the round glaring eyes, and at the moving wrinkles and long hairs on Master Spiderman's face, and he felt as much sick as he was frightened.

"*And* you promised us some food when we'd done it," he added.

Master Spiderman ignored this, but he seemed to control his rage a little. "For this spell," he said, in that way he had of almost talking to himself. There were little flecks of white around his wide, lipless mouth. "For this spell, I have kept myself alive for countless years beyond my natural span. This spell will change the world. This spell will *give* me the world! And one miserable boy nearly ruins it by trying to sweep it off the wall!"

"I didn't know it was a spell," Tonino protested. "What is it supposed to do?"

Master Spiderman laughed—a private sort of

laugh, with his mouth closed as if he were shutting in secrets. "Supposed?" he said. "It is *supposed* to make a *ten*-lifed enchanter, who is to be more powerful than any of your Chrestomancis. It *will* do so, as long as neither of you meddles with it again. Don't dare *touch* it!"

He stepped around them and made gestures at the wall, rather as if he were plaiting or twisting something. The gray swath of cobweb that Tonino had brought down billowed itself and lifted upward. Master Spiderman made flattening and twiddling motions with his hands then, and the cobwebs began moving this way and that, growing thicker as they moved, and wafting themselves up to stick to the ceiling. Cat thought he could see a host of little half-invisible creeping things scurrying about among the gray swath, repairing the spell the way Master Spiderman wanted it, and had to look away. Tonino, however, stared at them, amazed and interested.

"There," Master Spiderman said at last. "Don't go near it again." He turned to leave.

"Hang on," said Cat. "You promised us something to eat. Sir," he added quickly, as Master Spiderman swung angrily around at him. "We have cleaned the room, sir."

"I'll give you food," Master Spiderman said, "when you tell me which of you is Eric."

As before, the name meant nothing to either of them. But they were both so hungry by then that Cat instantly pointed to Tonino and Tonino just as promptly pointed at Cat. "He is," they said in chorus.

"I see," snapped Master Spiderman. "You don't know." He swung around again and hurried away, muttering to himself. The mutters turned into distinct speech while Master Spiderman was clambering up the steps. He must have thought they could not hear him from there. "I don't know which of you is either, damn it! I'll just have to kill both of you—one of you more than once, I imagine."

As the door shut with a boom, Cat and Tonino stared at one another, really frightened for the first time. "Let's try the window again," Cat said.

But the window still would not budge. Cat was standing on the workbench, wagging the broom handle out through the open space in hopes of breaking the spell on it, when he heard the door opening again. He came down hastily and kept hold of the broom for a weapon.

Master Spiderman came through the door with a lighted lamp, which he put down on the top step. They were glad to see the light. It was getting quite dark in the basement by then. They watched Master Spiderman turn and push a tray out onto the top step beside the lamp. "Here is your supper, boys," he said. "And here is what I want you to do next. Listen carefully. I want you to watch that spell at the end of the room. Don't take your eyes off it. And the moment you see anything different about it, you are to come and knock on the door and tell me. Do that, and you shall have a currant cake each as a reward."

There was a sort of oily friendliness about Master Spiderman now that made both boys very uneasy. Cat nudged Tonino, and Tonino at once began trying to find out what this new friendliness was about. "What are you expecting to happen to the spell?" he asked, looking very earnest and innocent.

"So we know what to look for," Cat explained.

Master Spiderman hesitated, obviously wondering what to tell them. "You will see a disturbance," he said. "Yes, a disturbance among the webs. It will look quite strange, but you must not be frightened. It will only be the soul of an enchanter who is presently on his deathbed, and it will, almost at once, turn harmlessly into a bean.

Make sure that the bean has dropped correctly into the container on the bench and then tell me. Then you shall each have a currant cake. You will do that and you shall have a cake each. You are good boys, are you not?"

"Oh, yes," they both assured him.

"Good." Master Spiderman backed out through the door and shut it again.

Cat and Tonino went cautiously up the stairs to look at the tray. On it were a tin jug of water, a small stale loaf, and a block of cheese so old and sweaty that it looked like a piece of soap someone had just washed with.

"Do you think it's poisoned?" Tonino whispered.

Cat thought about it. In a way it was a triumph that they had forced Master Spiderman to give them anything to eat, but it was quite plain that, even so, Master Spiderman was not going to waste decent food on people he was planning to kill. Giving them this food was just to lull them. "No," Cat said. "He'd use better food. I bet it's the currant cakes that are going to be poisoned."

Tonino was evidently thinking as well, while they carried the lamp and the tray down the steps and set both up on a workbench in the middle of the room. "He said," he observed, "that he has kept himself alive much longer than his normal lifetime. Do you think he does this by killing boys—his apprentices?"

Cat dragged the two least rickety chairs up beside the bench. "I don't know," he said, "but he might. I think when that enchanter's ghost gets here, we ought to ask it to help."

"A good idea," said Tonino. Then he added dubiously, "If it *can*."

"Of course it can," Cat said. "He'll still be an enchanter even if he *is* a ghost."

They tore the hard bread into lumps and set to work to gnaw at these and the rubbery cheese, taking it in turns to swig water out of the tin jug. The water tasted stale and pondlike. Cat's stomach began to hurt almost at once. Perhaps, he thought, his reasoning had been wrong, and this nasty supper was poisoned after all. On the other hand, it could be that this food was simply indigestible—or just that the mere idea of poison had made his stomach think it *was*.

He watched Tonino carefully to see if he was showing any signs of poisoning. But Tonino evidently trusted Cat's judgment. Under the soft lamplight, Tonino's eyes became brighter as he ate, and his dirty, drawn-looking cheeks became rounder and pinker. Cat watched him use his teeth to scrape the very last of the cheese off the rind and decided that there was no poison in this food. His stomach unclenched a little.

"I'm still hungry," Tonino said, laying the rind down regretfully. "I'm so hungry I could even eat those dry beans."

Cat remembered that he had crammed those beans into his pocket when Master Spiderman had come charging down the steps. He fetched them out and laid all seven under the lamp. He was surprised to see that they were glossier and plumper than they had been. Four of them had lost their wrinkles entirely. Even the oldest and most withered one looked more like a bean and less like a dried brown lump. They glowed soft reds and purples under the light. "I wonder," he said, pushing at them with a finger. "I wonder if these are all enchanters, too."

"They might be," Tonino said, staring at them. "He said he was to make a ten-lifed enchanter. Here might be seven lives, with an eighth one coming soon. Where does he get the other two lives from, though?"

From us, Cat thought, and hoped that Tonino would not think of this, too.

But at that moment the newest and glossiest bean gave a sudden jump and flipped over, end to end. Tonino forgot what they had been talking about and leaned over it, fascinated. "This one is alive! Are all the others living, too?"

It seemed that they were. One by one, each of the beans stirred and then flipped, until they were all rolling and hopping about, even the oldest bean, although this one only seemed to be able to rock from side to side. The newest bean was now flipping so vigorously that it nearly jumped off the workbench. Cat caught it and put it back among the others. "I wonder if they're going to grow," he said.

"Beanstalks," Tonino said. "Oh, please, yes!"

As he spoke, the newest bean split down its length to show a pale, greenish interior, which was clearly very much alive. But it was not so much like a bean growing. It was more like a beetle spreading its wings. For an instant the boys could see the two mottled purplish red halves of its skin, spread out like wing covers, and then these seemed to melt into the rest of it. What spread out then was a pale, greenish, transparent growing thing. The growing thing very quickly spread into a flatness with several points, until it looked like nothing so much as a large floating sycamore leaf made of greenish light. There were delicate veins in it and it pulsed slightly.

By this time five of the others were splitting and spreading, too. Each grew points and veins, but in slightly different shapes, so that Cat thought of them as an ivy leaf, a fig leaf, a vine leaf, a maple leaf, and a leaf from a plane tree. Even the oldest seventh bean was trying to split. But it was so withered and hard and evidently having such difficulty that Tonino put a forefinger on each half of it and helped it break open. "Oh, enchanters, please help us!" he said, as the bean spread into a smaller, more stunted shape.

Wild service tree leaf, Cat thought, and wondered a little how he knew about trees. He looked sadly at the cluster of frail, quivering, greenish shapes gathered by the base of the lamp and realized that Tonino had been right to be doubtful in the first place. The green shapes might once have been enchanters—Cat thought Tonino was right about that—but they were not ghosts. These beings were soft, helpless and bewildered. It was like asking newly hatched butterflies for help.

"I don't think they *can* help," he said. "They don't even know what's happened to them."

Tonino sighed. "They do feel awfully old," he agreed. "But they feel new, too. We shall have to help them instead. Make them hide from Master Spiderman."

He tried to catch the old, stunted leaf, but it fluttered away from his fingers, frantically. This seemed to alarm the rest. They all fluttered and trembled and moved in a glowing group to safety behind the tin jug.

"Leave off! You're frightening them!" Cat said. As he said it, he heard a sort of scuffling from behind him, at the end of the room. He and Tonino both whipped around to look.

There, glowing faintly among the draped cobwebs, another leaf-shaped thing, a big one, was struggling among the clinging, dusty threads. It was struggling even more frantically than the stunted leaf had struggled to get away from Tonino, but every flap and wriggle only brought it farther into the midst of the tangled webs and lower and lower toward the black canister.

"This is the dead enchanter!" Tonino said. "Oh, quickly! Help it!"

Cat got up slowly. He was rather afraid of the thing. It was like the times when a bird gets into your bedroom—a panic that was desperately catching—but when he saw the thing suddenly turn into a bean and plummet toward the black canister, he raced to the end of the room and pushed his hands nervously into the gray tangled shrouds of cobweb. He was just in time to deflect it with the edge of his left hand. The bean pinged against the canister and bounced out onto the floor. Cat scooped it up. The instant it was in his hand, the bean split and grew and became a bigger, brighter, and more pointed leaf shape than any of the others. Cat carried it, whirring between his hands, and deposited it carefully beside the rest, where it lay beside the others as part of a transparent, pulsing, living group, shining under the lamp. Like a shoal of fish, Cat thought.

"He's coming!" gasped Tonino. "Make them escape!"

Cat heard the door at the top of the steps opening. He flapped his hands at the cluster of leaf shapes. "Shoo!" he whispered. "Hide some-where!" All the leaf shapes flinched from his hands but, maddeningly, they all stayed where they were, hovering behind the tin jug.

"Oh, *go!*" Tonino implored them as Master Spiderman came storming down the steps. But they would not move.

"What are you boys playing at?" Master Spiderman demanded. He went hurrying through the room toward the draped cobwebs. "According to my star chart, Gabriel de Witt died nearly twenty minutes ago. His soul must have arrived here by now. Why have you not knocked on the door? Are you too busy feeding your faces to notice? Is that it?"

He stormed past the lamp and the workbench without looking at them. All the leaf shapes flinched as the angry gust of his passing hit them. Then, to Cat's extreme relief, the big new leaf shape lifted one side of itself in a sort of beckoning gesture and slid quietly over the edge of the bench into the shadows underneath it. The others turned themselves and flitted after it, like a row of flatfish diving, with the old, stunted one hastening after in last place. Cat and Tonino turned their eyes sideways to make sure they were hidden and then looked quickly back at Master Spiderman. He was hurling cobwebs right and left in order to get at the black canister.

He snatched it up. He shook it. He turned around, clutching it to his chest, in such amazement and despair that Cat almost felt sorry for him. "It's empty!" he said. His face was the face of the saddest monkey in the most unkind zoo in any world. "Empty!" he repeated. "All gone—all the souls I have collected are gone! The souls of seven nine-lifed enchanters are missing, and the new one is not here! My lifetime's work! What has gone wrong?" As he asked this, the grief in his face hardened suddenly to anger and suspicion. "What have you boys done?"

Cat had been prepared to feel very frightened when Master Spiderman realized it was their fault. He was slightly surprised to feel more tense than frightened and quite businesslike. It was a great help to have Tonino opposite him, looking calm and sturdy. "They got out," he said.

"They started to grow," Tonino said. "They were beans, you know, and beans grow. Why are you upset, sir? Were you meaning to swallow them?"

"Of *course* I was!" Master Spiderman more or less howled. "I have been intercepting the souls of dead Chrestomancis for more than two hundred *years*, you stupid little boy! When there were nine, and I swallowed them, I would be the strongest enchanter there has ever been! And you let them get out!"

"But there were only eight," Tonino pointed out.

Master Spiderman hugged the canister to himself and spread his mouth into a wide smile. "No," he said. "Nine. One of you boys has my ninth soul, and the other eight have no way to get out of this room." And he shouted, loudly and suddenly, *"Where have they gone?"*

Cat and Tonino both jumped and tried to look as if they had no idea. But the shout obviously terrified the dead souls lurking under the table. One of the middle-size ones, the one like a fig leaf, made a dash for freedom, between the broken rungs of Cat's chair and out toward the stairs and the open door at the top. The others all followed an instant later, as if they could not bear to be left behind, streaming after it in a luminous line.

"Aha!" shouted Master Spiderman. He dropped the canister and ran at an incredible speed through the room and up the first three stairs, where he was just in time to block the path of the escaping souls. Above him the door banged shut. The line of leaf shapes swirled to a stop almost level with the lowest stair, where they dithered in the air a little and then darted away sideways with the big new soul in the lead and the smallest, oldest one fluttering rather desperately in the rear.

At this, Master Spiderman leaped down the steps and snatched up a butterfly net from the heap of rubbish. "Lively, are you?" he muttered. "Soon put a stop to that!" Two more butterfly nets left the heap and planted themselves, one in Cat's hand and one in Tonino's. "You let them out," he said. "You get them caught again." And with that, he went leaping after the streaming line of souls with his butterfly net held sideways to scoop them up.

Cat and Tonino jumped up and began pretending to chase the fleeing souls, too, getting in Master Spiderman's way whenever they could. Tonino galumphed backward and forward, waving his net and shouting, "Got you!" and "Oh, bother, I *missed!*" in all the wrong places and particularly when he was nowhere near the streaming line of souls. Cat sprinted beside Master Spiderman, and whenever Master Spiderman lunged to scoop up the souls, Cat made sure to lunge, too, and either to jog Master Spiderman's elbow or to cross Master Spiderman's butterfly net with his own so that he missed.

Master Spiderman howled and snarled at him, but he was too intent on catching the souls to do anything to Cat. Around the basement they sped, like people in a mad game of lacrosse, with

Tonino galloping in the middle, upsetting broken furniture into their path, while the line of shining, desperately frightened souls sped around the room at waist level, swerved outward to miss the draped cobwebs, and rushed along the wall with the window in it, slightly higher up.

Window! Cat thought at them as he chased beside Master Spiderman. Window's open! But they were too frightened to notice the window and streamed on toward the steps again. There the ivy leaf soul must have had the idea that the door was still open and tried to dart up the steps. The others all stopped and swirled around to follow it.

Seeing this, Master Spiderman shouted, "Aha!" again and rushed toward them with his net ready. Cat and Tonino had to do some fast and artistic jumping about on the stairs, or the whole lot would have been scooped up there and then.

Then separate, you fools! Cat thought. Why don't you all fly different ways?

But this, it seemed, the terrified souls could not bear to do. Cat could feel them thinking that they would be lost if they were alone. They streamed on in a cluster, up into the corner of the room and then on around it again, just below the ceiling, with Master Spiderman close behind, net raised, and Cat pelting after him. There was a heart-stopping moment then when the old, small soul flew too near the draped cobwebs and got tangled in them. Again the other souls swirled to a stop and waited. Cat only got there just in time. Butterfly nets clashed as Cat managed to stumble into the cobwebs and carve them apart to let the trapped soul loose.

As it went fluttering after the others, Tonino galloped across the room and squeezed behind the bench that Cat had stood on to open the window. The bench went over with a crash. The line of souls had just gathered speed again, but this brought them almost to a standstill. Tonino stood waving his net back and forth beside the window, trying to give them a hint.

The souls understood—or at least the big new one that had been Gabriel de Witt seemed to. It made for the window in a glad swoop. The luminous green line of the others followed and all went whirling out through the gap into the dark night as if they had been sucked out by the draft.

Thank goodness! Cat thought, leaning on his butterfly net and panting. Now he won't need to kill us either.

Master Spiderman uttered a great scream of

rage. "You opened the window! You broke my spells!" He made a throwing motion toward Cat and then at Tonino. Cat felt a light, strong stickiness close about him. He had barely time to think that it felt remarkably like when you brush through a cobweb by accident before Master Spiderman was rushing up the basement steps. Cat and Tonino, sweaty and breathless and covered with dirt as they were, found they were forced to rush up the steps behind him.

"I am not letting you out of my sight from now on!" Master Spiderman panted as they pelted through the room overhead. They were going too fast for Tonino, who nearly fell on his face as they reached the hallway. Cat dragged him upright while Master Spiderman was hurling open the front door, and they pelted on, out into the street. It was pitch-dark out there. Curtains were drawn over the windows of all the houses and there were no kinds of streetlights anywhere. Master Spiderman stopped, panting heavily, and seemed to be staring wildly around.

For a second or so Cat had hopes that the escaped souls had got away, or at least had had the sense to hide.

But the souls had no sense. They did not have

proper brains to have sense *with*, Cat thought sadly. They were hovering in a little cluster at the end of the street, just as greenly luminous and easy to see as they had been in the basement, and bobbing anxiously together as if they were discussing what to do now.

"There!" Master Spiderman cried out triumphantly. He dived down the street, nearly pulling Cat and Tonino over.

"Oh, fly away! Go somewhere safe!" Tonino panted as they stumbled on down the pavement.

The souls saw them at the last possible moment—or they made up their nonminds what to do, Cat was not sure which. At all events, as Master Spiderman's butterfly net was sweeping toward them, they swirled upward in a spiral, with the big soul that had been Gabriel de Witt's leading, and vanished across the roof of the house on the corner.

Master Spiderman screamed with frustration and rose into the air, too. Cat and Tonino were lugged up into the air after him, spinning and dangling sideways. Before they could right themselves, they were being towed across chimney pots and roofs at a furious speed.

By the time Cat had hauled on Tonino and

Tonino had clutched at Cat, and they had discovered that they could use the butterfly nets they still held to balance themselves upright in the air, they were going even faster, with the wind of speed in their eyes and whipping at their hair. They could see the small green cluster of souls fleeing ahead of them above a ragged field with donkeys in it and then above a wood. There was a big half-moon that Cat had not noticed before, lying on its back among clouds, which served to show the souls up even more bright and green.

"Faster!" Master Spiderman snapped, as they all hurtled across the wood, too.

"Go as fast as he does, go as fast as he does," Cat heard Tonino whisper.

This was exactly what seemed to happen. Master Spiderman snapped, "Faster!" several times, once when the moon vanished and there were suddenly a thousand more roofs and chimneys whirling beneath them, again when it came on to rain briefly, and yet again when there was a full moon shining down on some kind of park below. Yet the small green cluster of souls speeding ahead stayed precisely the same distance in front of them. The dark landscape underneath changed again, but they were still no nearer, and no farther away either.

"Curses!" panted Master Spiderman. "They're traveling into the future. This is a hundred and fifty years now. Boys, give me your strength. I command it!"

Cat felt energy draining strongly out of him through the invisible cobwebs that were towing him after Master Spiderman. Although this was not a pleasant feeling, it seemed to lift some of the fuzzy blankness in his mind. Cat found dim memories flitting through his head as they sped on, of faces and places mostly—a castle, a handsome dark-haired man saying something sarcastic, a lady in mittens, a very old man lying in bed. And a smell. Around the very old man in bed there had hung the same musty, sick smell that came strongly, in gusts, off Master Spiderman as he whirled along in front. But Cat could not put these memories together to make sense. It was easier to notice that the chimney pots beneath now seemed to be growing out into the countryside, in lines along the sides of fields, and to listen to Tonino, who was still whispering, "Go as fast as we do, go as fast as we do!" over and over.

"Are you using his spell or something?" Cat whispered.

"I think so," Tonino whispered back. "I seem to remember doing this before."

Cat seemed to remember Tonino could do this sort of thing, too, but before he could discover how he knew, the landscape below jerked into another different shape. There were handsome gas streetlights down there now, trees lining wide roads and houses that stood apart from one another in gardens. Ahead, the small glowing group of souls hurtled across a village green and then over a dimly gleaming railway line.

"I *know* this place!" Cat said. "I think we were here this morning."

Almost at the same time, Master Spiderman was making confused noises. "I thought he was taking them to his home," he said, "but we have passed it. Where are they *going* then?"

In front of them, the souls streamed above some tall trees and almost instantly dived down beyond, toward a tall building with rows of lighted windows. Still making puzzled noises and grunting with the effort, Master Spiderman dragged himself and Cat and Tonino across the treetops after them.

They were in time to see the souls, in a luminous line with the big one still leading, go streaming sedately in through the big arched door in the middle of the building. At the sight, Master Spiderman yelled with rage and plunged them all downward so quickly that Cat had to shut his eyes. It was even quicker than falling.

They landed with a fairly violent bump on what was luckily a soft lawn. Tonino and Cat got up quickly, but Master Spiderman was winded and staggered about gasping, looking so thin and bent and hollow-faced that he might almost have been a real monkey. They could see him clearly, propping himself on his butterfly net and puffing, because there was a large light over the arched door of the building. The light shone on letters carved into the stone of the arch: HOSPITAL OF THE SACRED HEART.

"A *hospital!*" Master Spiderman panted. "Why would they want to come *here*? Don't stand there staring, you stupid boys! We have to catch them!" And he was off again, using the butterfly net like a walking stick and muttering, "Oh, *why* do I always get so *old* when I come to the future? Come on, you wretched boys, come *on!*"

He dragged them in through the doorway into a most obvious hospital corridor, long, pale green, and well lit, and smelling so strongly of antiseptic that it drowned even the smell of Master Spiderman. Cat and Tonino both became extremely conscious of how dirty they were. They tried to hang back. But there near the end of the corridor, almost transparent yellow in the strong light, was the little cluster of souls, floating nervously near a staircase, as if they were again undecided what to do. The sight seemed to inspire Master Spiderman to a second wind. He broke into a gallop, waving his butterfly net, and the boys were dragged into a gallop, too.

When they were halfway along the corridor, a nun came out of a doorway, carrying a kidney dish. She was one of those nuns with a headdress that was made of big starched points, like a ship in full sail.

Not a headdress to dodge in, Cat would have thought. But dodge she did as Master Spiderman came charging down on her like a wild monkey in a flying black coat, with Cat and Tonino helplessly sprinting behind him. The nun's headdress gave an outraged rattle, and she backed into a doorway, clutching her kidney dish and staring as they all rushed past.

The souls saw them coming and made up their minds. The big one darted for the staircase, and the others went streaming after, up alongside the crisp green line painted on the wall. Master Spiderman hopped on one foot in order to stop, spun around, and went hammering up the stairs behind them. So, perforce, did Cat and Tonino.

As they all got to the top, another nun was just coming through a swing door, holding it open with her back so that she could wrestle a big tray with bottles on it through the door, too. The souls swirled neatly around her huge starched headdress and on into the ward beyond. The nun did not see them. But she saw Master Spiderman with his face stretched into a grin of effort bounding toward the door like a maniac monkey, and the two dirty, perspiring, cobwebby boys behind him. She dropped the tray and screamed.

Master Spiderman barged her aside and dashed into the ward, dragging the boys with him.

They were in a long, dimly lighted space with a row of beds on either side. The souls were about halfway down the room, flitting cautiously in their usual cluster. But the place was not quiet. Cat had the strange feeling that they had just burst into a rookery. The air rang with peculiar cawing noises.

It took him a second or so to realize that the cawing was coming from little white cradles that were hooked to the bottom of each bed. All the people in the beds were ladies, all looking rather exhausted, and in each cradle there was a tiny, wrinkly, red-faced newborn baby—at least, there were two of them in the cradle nearest Cat—and it was the babies who were making the noise, more and more of them, as the nun's scream and the crash of the bottles, followed by the thunder of the door and the shout of anger Master Spiderman gave as he towed Cat and Tonino between the beds, woke every single baby there up.

"We're in a maternity ward," Cat said, wishing he could back straight out of here again.

Tonino was horribly out of breath, but he managed to grin. "I know. The souls are being clever after all."

Master Spiderman was shouting, "Stop them! Don't let them get into any babies! They'll be gone for good then!" He dived at the cluster of souls with his butterfly net raised.

The souls did seem to be showing intelligence at last. As Master Spiderman dived, they rose up in a group above his waving net and then peeled apart in eight different directions. For a second or so, Master Spiderman did manage to keep most of them up in the air by swatting at them and shouting, but then two dived over behind him.

Like a pair of shooting stars, the ivy leaf and the fig leaf shot downward to two of the cradles. Each poised for a moment over a yelling baby and then softly descended into the baby's wide-open bawling mouth. And were gone. A look of acute surprise crossed the face of each baby. Then they were yelling louder than ever with their faces screwed up and their short arms batting the air. It must feel very strange, Cat thought, suddenly to find you had two souls, but he could not see that it did any harm. And it was the perfect place to hide from Master Spiderman.

He nudged Tonino. "I think we'd better help them."

Tonino nodded. They set off down the ward just as things began to get difficult. Master Spiderman was speeding this way and that, scooping at darting souls, and most of the new mothers, tired as they were, were beginning to sit up and object. They could not seem to see the souls, but they could see Master Spiderman.

"What do you think you're doing?" several ladies demanded.

Another said, "I'm not letting that madman near my baby!" She picked her howling baby out of its cradle, just as the fluttering maple leaf soul was poised above it, and hugged it to her chest. The maple leaf was forced to swoop on to the next cradle, where Master Spiderman's butterfly net scooped at it and missed.

"He's a lunatic," said the mother in the next bed. "Ring the bell for help."

"I already did," said a mother in the bed opposite. "I rang twice now."

"It's too bad!" several mothers said. And several more shouted at Master Spiderman to get out or they would have the law on him.

Meanwhile soul after soul darted away from Master Spiderman and vanished into babies. By this time only two were left, the oldest and the newest. The oldest leaf was still stunted, though it seemed to have grown a little, but it was evidently bewildered and weak. All its efforts to get into babies were timid and slow, and whenever Master Spiderman's butterfly net swept toward it, all it seemed able to do was to flutter up toward the ceiling again, where the newest and biggest leaf shape hovered, perhaps trying to tell the old leaf what to do.

The old soul timorously descended again as Cat and Tonino set off to help it. Master

Spiderman pelted back to catch it. But he skidded to a stop when the ward doors clapped open, and an awesome voice asked, "And what, pray, is the meaning of this?"

It was the Mother Superior. It did not take the hugeness of her starched headdress, the severity of her dark blue habit, the large silver cross hanging from her waist, or even her six feet of height to tell you who and what she was. It was obvious. Such was the power of her personality that as she advanced down the ward, nearly all the babies stopped crying.

The big soul that had been Gabriel de Witt hastily plunged from near the ceiling and was just in time to vanish into the only baby still crying. The mothers who were sitting up all hurriedly lay down again, and the one who had picked her baby up guiltily popped it back into its cradle and lay down, too. Cat and Tonino, feeling as guilty as the rest, stood still and tried to look as if they were visiting a new little brother or sister. Master Spiderman's flat mouth hung open as if the Mother Superior had cast a spell on him. But Cat did not think it was magic. As the Mother Superior's cold eye passed over him, he knew it was pure personality. He wanted to sink into the floor.

"I do not," said the Mother Superior to Master Spiderman, "wish to know what you are doing here, my good man. I want you simply to take your butterfly net and your filthy street urchins, and leave. Now."

"Very good, ma'am." Master Spiderman cringed. His hairy monkey face twisted with guilt. For an instant it seemed as if he were going to do as he was told and go away. But the stunted and bewildered old soul, which had been hovering miserably up near the ceiling, suddenly decided that the Mother Superior was the one to keep it safe. It came down in a fluttering spiral and landed on her great white headdress, where it nestled, frail and quivering, upon the highest starched point. Master Spiderman stared at it urgently, with round monkey eyes.

"Off you go," said the Mother Superior, "my good man."

Master Spiderman's face bunched up. "I'll have this one at least," Cat heard him mutter. He made one of his throwing gestures. "Freeze," he said.

The Mother Superior promptly became as stiff and still as a statue. Most of the babies started to cry again.

"Good," said Master Spiderman. "I never did

hold with nuns. Nasty religious creatures." He stood on tiptoe to swat the roosting old soul into his net. But the Mother Superior's headdress was just too high for him. It flapped and rattled as he hit it, and the Mother Superior herself swayed about, and the soul, instead of being swatted into the net, was shot off sideways into the cradle that contained the twins. Both were bawling just then.

Cat saw the soul dive thankfully, but he did not see which twin got it, because Master Spiderman pushed him angrily aside and tried to unhook the cradle from the bed. "I'll have this one at least!" he cried out. "I'll start all over again, but I'll have *one!*"

"You will *not!*" said the mother of the twins. She climbed out of bed and advanced on Master Spiderman. She was enormous. She had huge arms that looked as if they had plowed and reaped fields, made dough, and pounded washing clean until they were stronger than the arms of most men. The rest of her was in a vast white night-gown with a frill around its neck, and on top of the frill was a surprisingly pretty and very deter-mined face.

Cat took one look at her and respectfully handed her his butterfly net as she marched past him. She gave him a nod of thanks and absently turned it back to front, with the net near her hand. "Let go that cradle," she said, "or I shall make you very sorry."

Master Spiderman hastily hooked the cradle onto the bed again and backed away. "Let's be reasonable here, madam," he said in his most oily and placating manner. "You have two fine babies there. Suppose I were to give you a gold piece for the pair of them."

"I never," said the huge lady, "heard anything so disgusting in my life!" And she swung the shaft of the butterfly net with both hands.

Master Spiderman had just time to yell. "*Two* gold pieces then!" before the handle of the net met his head with a whistling crack. His hat came off, revealing his wispy brown scalp, and he tottered sideways, shrieking. Tottered some more and fell against the Mother Superior. Cat and Tonino were just in time to hold her upright by leaning against her as Master Spiderman slid howling down the front of her.

And as he slid, his bare head hit the silver cross hanging from the Mother Superior's waist. There was a strange crackling sound, followed by a strong smell. Master Spiderman jerked all over and hit the floor with an empty sort of flop. Cat found himself staring down at an old brown dead thing, that was so dried out and so withered that it might have been a mummified monkey. It looked as if it had died centuries before.

Cat's first act was to look anxiously around for any sign of Master Spiderman's soul. He did not want that getting into a baby. But it seemed almost as if any soul Master Spiderman had had was gone long ago. He could see and feel nothing of it. Then he looked down at the brown mummified thing again and thought, shuddering, If that's an evil enchanter, I don't want to be anything like *that*! At which point, he found he remembered who he was and that he was an enchanter, too. And he was suddenly so engulfed in feelings and memories that he could not move.

Around him the babies were all crying at full strength, and most of their mothers were cheering. The mother of the twins was sitting on her bed saying she felt rather queer.

"I'm not surprised!" said the Mother Superior. "You did very well, my dear. A good flush hit—one of the best I've ever seen."

On the other side of the Mother Superior, Tonino was doing what Cat realized he should have been doing hours ago and shouting at the top of his strong, clear voice, "Chrestomanci! Chrestomanci, come here quickly!"

There was a blat of warm moving air, like a train passing, combined with a strange spicy smell from another universe entirely, and Chrestomanci was standing in the ward, almost face-to-face with the Mother Superior.

The effect was extremely odd. The Conclave of Mages seemed to require Chrestomanci to wear a skinny thigh-length white tunic above enormously baggy black trousers. It made him look even taller than the Mother Superior, and a great deal thinner.

"Ah, Mother Janissary," he said. "Good evening. We met last year, I believe."

"At the canonical conference, and my name is Mother Justinia," the Mother Superior replied. "I am extremely glad to see you, Sir Christopher. We seem to have a spot of bother here."

"So I see," said Chrestomanci. He looked down at the remains of Master Spiderman and then across at Cat and Tonino. After that, his gaze traveled around the ward, the howling babies and the staring mothers, and he began to get his most bewildered look. "It seems a little late in the day for hospital visiting," he said. "Perhaps someone will tell me why we are all here." His brow creased and he made a little gesture, at which all the babies stopped crying and fell peacefully asleep. "That's better," he said. "Tonino, you explain."

Tonino told it, clearly and well. There were several occasions when Cat might have interrupted with some further explanations, but he scarcely said anything, because he was so ashamed. It was not just that he, a nine-lifed enchanter, had let Master Spiderman cast a spell on him to make him forget what he was—and he knew he should have noticed the spell; it must have been inside that old hackney cab—but the fact that he, Cat, had been so busy resenting Tonino that he had nearly got both of them killed.

It made him feel worse that Tonino kept saying that Cat had behaved well and that Cat had been managing to work magic in spite of Master Spiderman's spells. Cat did not think either of these things was true. The most he could say for himself was he was glad he had been sorry for the trapped souls, enough to help rescue them. And he supposed he was glad to find he liked Tonino after all. Tonino had been so calm and sturdy through it all—the perfect companion. And he suspected that Tonino's backup magic had done twice as much as his own.

"So Gabriel de Witt is dead," Chrestomanci said sadly.

"Not really," Tonino said, gesturing around at the sleeping babies. "He is here somewhere."

"Ah, yes, but I imagine he—or she—doesn't know who he is now," Chrestomanci answered. He sighed. "So Neville Spiderman was hiding out in a time bubble, collecting the souls of all the Chrestomancis, was he? And probably killing apprentices to prolong his own life while he waited. It was lucky he kidnapped the two of you. We'd never have caught him without that. But now we have, I think we'd better get rid of what's left of him; it looks infectious to me. How old is this hospital?" he asked the Mother Superior.

"About seventy years old," she replied, rather surprised.

"And what was here before it was built, do you know?" Chrestomanci asked.

She shrugged, rattling her headdress. "Just green fields, I think."

"Good," said Chrestomanci. "Then I can send him back in time without moving him. It's a bit hard on the person who falls over him in the field, but it fits with what I remember. He was supposed to have been found dead in a ditch somewhere near Dulwich. Will everyone please stand back?"

Cat, Tonino, and Mother Justinia all backed away a pace. Before they had quite finished moving, a blue glow appeared around the monkeylike thing on the floor, and Neville Spiderman was gone. This was followed by a rapidly evaporating puddle with a strong smell of hospital.

"Disinfectant," Chrestomanci explained. "Now, we have eight souls to account for still. Cat, can you remember which babies they all went to?"

Cat was more ashamed than ever. The babies all looked alike to him. And it had all been so confusing, with souls darting in all directions. "I've no idea," he confessed. "One of the twins, but I don't know which. And that's all."

"They all went everywhere," Tonino explained. "Won't their mothers know?"

"Most people," said Chrestomanci, "can't see souls. It takes magic. Oh, well. We'll have to do it the hard way."

He turned around and snapped his fingers. The young man who acted as Chrestomanci's secretary jumped into existence farther up the ward. He was obviously not used to this kind of summons. He was in the middle of tying a spotted bow tie and almost dropped it. Cat could see him staring around at the mothers, the babies, and the Mother Superior and then at the filthy and disheveled boys, and trying to look as if he saw such things every day.

"Tom," Chrestomanci said to him, "be a good fellow and go around and get the names and addresses of all the mothers and every baby here, will you?"

"Certainly, sir," Tom said, trying to look efficient and understanding.

Some of the mothers looked indignant at this, and Mother Justinia said, "Is that really necessary? We like to be confidential here."

"Absolutely necessary," Chrestomanci said. He raised his voice so that all the mothers could hear him. "Some of your babies are going to grow up with very powerful magic. They might have strange memories, too, which could frighten both you and them. We want to be able to help them if this happens. We also want to educate them properly in the use of their magic. But since none of us knows *which* children are going to have these gifts, we are going to have to keep track of you all. So we are going to give each baby here a government grant of five hundred pounds a year until he or she is eighteen. Does this make you feel better about it?"

"You mean they get the money if they have magic or not?" somebody asked.

"Exactly," said Chrestomanci. "Of course they only get the grant when they come to Chrestomanci Castle once a year for magical testing."

"Mine might have magic anyway," someone else murmured. "My mother's father—"

The twins' mother said, "Well, I'm taking the money. I was at my wits' end how to give them all they need. I wasn't reckoning on twins. Thank you, sir."

"My pleasure, madam," Chrestomanci said, bowing to her. "Tom will give you any further details." Tom, who had just conjured himself a notebook and a pen, looked pleading and alarmed at this. Chrestomanci ignored him. "He can cope," he said to Cat. "That's what he's paid for. You and Tonino look as if you need a bath and a square meal. Let's take you both home."

"But—" said Cat.

"But what?" asked Chrestomanci.

Cat did not know how to put the shame he felt. He was fairly sure he had been starting to turn into someone like Neville Spiderman, but he did not dare tell Chrestomanci that. "I don't deserve anything," he said.

"No more than those twins deserve five hundred pounds a year each," Chrestomanci said cheerfully. "I don't know what's biting you, Cat, but it seems to me that you've managed rather well in a dangerous situation without thinking you can rely on magic to help you. Think about it."

Beside Cat, Tonino exclaimed. Cat looked up from the floor to find they were in the grand central hall of Chrestomanci Castle, standing in the five-pointed star under the chandelier. Millie was rushing down the marble stairs to meet them.

"Oh, you *found* them!" she called out. "I've been so worried. Mordecai telephoned to say he put them in a cab that disappeared at the end of the street. He was terribly upset. And Gabriel de Witt died this evening, did you hear?"

"After a fashion," Chrestomanci said. "In one way Gabriel's still very much with us." He looked from Millie to Cat and Tonino. "Dear, dear. Everyone looks exhausted. I tell you what. I can borrow a villa in the south of France once the measles have abated—with a swimming pool. Tonino can go on to Italy from there. Would you like that, Tonino?"

"Yes, but I cannot swim," Tonino said.

"Neither can I," Cat said. "But we can both learn."

Tonino beamed at him and Cat was glad to discover he still liked Tonino, rather a lot.

CAROL ONEIR'S HUNDREDTH DREAM

CAROL ONEIR WAS the world's youngest best-selling dreamer. The newspapers called her the Infant Genius. Her photograph appeared regularly in all the daily papers and monthly magazines, either sitting alone in an armchair looking soulful or nestling lovingly against her mama.

Mama was very proud of Carol. So were Carol's publishers, Wizard Reverie Ltd. They marketed her product in big bright blue genie jars tied with cherry-colored satin ribbon; but you could also buy the Carol Oneir Omnibus Pillow, bright pink and heart-shaped, Carol's Dreamie Comics, the Carol Oneir Dream Hatband, the Carol Oneir Charm Bracelet, and half a hundred other spin-offs.

Carol had discovered at the age of seven that

she was one of those lucky people who can control what they dream about, and then loosen the dream in their minds so that a competent wizard can spin it off and bottle it for other people to enjoy. Carol loved dreaming. She had made no less than ninety-nine full-length dreams. She loved all the attention she got and all the expensive things her mama was able to buy for her. So it was a terrible blow to her when she lay down one night to start dreaming her hundredth dream and nothing happened at all.

It was a terrible blow to Mama, too, who had just ordered a champagne breakfast to celebrate Carol's Dream Century. Wizard Reverie Ltd. was just as upset as Mama. Its nice Mr. Ploys got up in the middle of the night and came down to Surrey by the milk train. He soothed Mama, and he soothed Carol, and he persuaded Carol to lie down and try to dream again. But Carol still could not dream. She tried every day for the following week, but she had no dreams at all, not even the kinds of dreams ordinary people have.

The only person who took it calmly was Dad. He went fishing as soon as the crisis started. Mr. Ploys and Mama took Carol to all the best doctors, in case Carol was overtired or ill. But she wasn't. So Mama took Carol up to Harley Street to consult Herman Mindelbaum, the famous mind wizard. But Mr. Mindelbaum could find nothing wrong either. He said Carol's mind was in perfect order and that her self-confidence was rather surprisingly high, considering.

In the car going home, Mama wept and Carol sobbed. Mr. Ploys said frantically, "Whatever happens, we mustn't let a *hint* of this get to the newspapers!" But of course it was too late. Next day the papers all had headlines saying CAROL ONEIR SEES MIND SPECIALIST and IS CAROL ALL DREAMED OUT? Mama burst into tears again, and Carol could not eat any breakfast.

Dad came home from fishing later that day to find reporters sitting in rows on the front steps. He prodded his way politely through them with his fishing rod, saying, "There is nothing to get excited about. My daughter is just very tired, and we're taking her to Switzerland for a rest." When he finally got indoors, he said, "We're in luck. I've managed to arrange for Carol to see an expert."

"Don't be silly, dear. We saw Mr. Mindelbaum yesterday," Mama sobbed.

"I know, dear. But I said an expert, not a specialist," said Dad. "You see, I used to be at school with Chrestomanci—once, long ago, when we were both younger than Carol. In fact, he lost his first life because I hit him around the head with a cricket bat. Now, of course, being a nine-lifed enchanter, he's a great deal more important than Carol is, and I had a lot of trouble getting hold of him. I was afraid he wouldn't want to remember me, but he did. He said he'd see Carol. The snag is, he's on holiday in the South of France, and he doesn't want the resort filling with newspaper-men—"

"I'll see to all that," Mr. Ploys cried joyfully. "Chrestomanci! Mr. Oneir, I'm *awed*. I'm struck dumb!"

Two days later Carol and her parents and Mr. Ploys boarded first-class sleepers in Calais on the Swiss Orient Express. The reporters boarded it, too, in second-class sleepers and third-class seats, and they were joined by French and German reporters standing in the corridors. The crowded train rattled away through France until, in the middle of the night, it came to Strasbourg, where a lot of shunting always went on. Carol's sleeper, with Carol and her parents asleep in it, was shunted off and hitched to the back of the Riviera Golden Arrow, and the Swiss Orient went on to Zurich without her.

Mr. Ploys went to Switzerland with it. He told Carol that, although he was really a dream wizard, he had skill enough to keep the reporters thinking Carol was still on the train. "If Chrestomanci wants to be private," he said, "it could cost me my job if I let one of these near him."

By the time the reporters discovered the deception, Carol and her parents had arrived in the seaside resort of Teignes on the French Riviera. There Dad—not without one or two wistful looks at the casino—unpacked his rods and went fishing. Mama and Carol took a horse-drawn cab up the hill to the private villa where Chrestomanci was staying.

They dressed in their best for the appointment. Neither of them had met anyone before who was more important than Carol. Carol wore ruched blue satin the same color as her genie bottles, with no less than three hand-embroidered lace petticoats underneath it. She had on matching button boots and a blue ribbon in her carefully curled hair, and she carried a blue satin parasol. She also wore her diamond heart pendant, her brooch that said CAROL in diamonds, her two sapphire bracelets, and all six of her gold bangles.

Her blue satin bag had diamond clasps in the shape of two C's. Mama was even more magnificent in a cherry-colored Paris gown, a pink hat, and all her emeralds.

They were shown up to a terrace by a rather plain lady who, as Mama whispered to Carol behind her fan, was really rather overdressed for a servant. Carol envied Mama her fan.

There were so many stairs to the terrace that she was too hot to speak when they got there. She let Mama exclaim at the wonderful view. You could see the sea and the beach and look into the streets of Teignes from here. As Mama said, the casino looked charming and the golf links so peaceful. On the other side, the villa had its own private swimming pool. This was full of splashing, screaming children, and to Carol's mind, it rather spoiled the view.

Chrestomanci was sitting reading in a deck chair. He looked up and blinked a little as they came. Then he seemed to remember who they were and stood up with great politeness to shake hands. He was wearing a beautifully tailored natural silk suit. Carol saw at a glance that it had cost at least as much as Mama's Paris gown. But her first thought on seeing Chrestomanci was, Oh, my! He's twice as good-looking as Francis! She pushed that thought down quickly and trod it under. It belonged to the thoughts she never even told Mama. But it meant that she rather despised Chrestomanci for being quite so tall and for having hair so black and such flashing dark eyes. She knew he was going to be no more help than Mr. Mindelbaum, and Mr. Mindelbaum had reminded her of Melville.

Mama meanwhile was holding Chrestomanci's hand between both of hers and saying, "Oh, sir! This is so good of you to interrupt your holiday on our account! But when even Mr. Mindelbaum couldn't find out what's stopping her dreams——"

"Not at all," Chrestomanci said, wrestling for his hand rather. "To be frank, I was intrigued by a case even Mindelbaum couldn't fathom." He signaled to the serving lady who had brought them to the terrace. "Millie, do you think you could take Mrs. . . . er . . . O'Dear downstairs while I talk to Carol?"

"There's no need for that, sir," Mama said, smiling. "I always go everywhere with my darling. Carol knows I'll sit quite quietly and not interrupt."

"No wonder Mindelbaum got nowhere,"

Chrestomanci murmured.

Then—Carol, who prided herself on being very observant, was never quite sure how it happened—Mama was suddenly not on the terrace anymore. Carol herself was sitting in a deck chair facing Chrestomanci in his deck chair, listening to Mama's voice floating up from below somewhere. "I never let Carol go anywhere alone. She's my one ewe lamb. . . ."

Chrestomanci leaned back comfortably and crossed his elegant legs. "Now," he said, "be kind enough to tell me exactly what you do when you make a dream."

This was something Carol had done hundreds of times by now. She smiled graciously and began, "I get a feeling in my head first, which means a dream is ready to happen. Dreams come when they will, you know, and there is no stopping them or putting them off. So I tell Mama, and we go up to my boudoir, where she helps me to get settled on the special couch Mr. Ploys had made for me. Then Mama sets the spin-off spool turning and tiptoes away, and I drop off to sleep to the sound of it gently humming and whirling. Then the dream takes me. . . ."

Chrestomanci did not take notes like Mr.

Mindelbaum and the reporters. He did not nod at her encouragingly the way Mr. Mindelbaum had. He simply stared vaguely out to sea. Carol thought that the least he might do was to tell those children in the pool to keep quiet. The screaming and splashing were so loud that she almost had to shout. Carol thought he was being very inconsiderate, but she kept on.

"I have learned not to be frightened and to go where the dream takes me. It is like a voyage of discovery—"

"When is this?" Chrestomanci interrupted in an offhand sort of way. "Does this dreaming happen at night?"

"It can happen at any time," said Carol. "If a dream is ready, I can go to my couch and sleep during the day."

"How very useful," murmured Chrestomanci. "So you can put up your hand in a dull lesson and say, 'Please can I be excused to go and dream?' Do they let you go home?"

"I ought to have explained," Carol said, keeping her dignity with an effort, "that Mama arranges lessons for me at home so that I can dream anytime I need to. It's like a voyage of discovery, sometimes in caves underground, sometimes in palaces in the clouds—"

"Yes. And how long do you dream for? Six hours? Ten minutes?" Chrestomanci interrupted again.

"About half an hour," said Carol. "Sometimes in the clouds or maybe in the southern seas. I never know where I will go or whom I will meet on my journey—"

"Do you finish a whole dream in half an hour?" Chrestomanci interrupted yet again.

"Of course not. Some of my dreams last for more than three hours," Carol said. "As for the people I meet, they are strange and wonderful—"

"So you dream in half-hour stretches," said Chrestomanci. "And I suppose you have to take a dream up again exactly where you left it at the end of the half hour before."

"Obviously," said Carol. "People must have told you: I can *control* my dreams. And I do my best work in regular half-hour stints. I wish you wouldn't keep interrupting when I'm doing my best to tell you!"

Chrestomanci turned his face from the sea and looked at her. He seemed surprised. "My dear young lady, you are *not* doing your best to tell me. I do read the papers, you know. You are giving me precisely the same flannel you gave the *Times* and the *Croydon Gazette* and the *People's Monthly* and doubtless poor Mindelbaum as well. You are telling me your dreams come unbidden—but you have one for half an hour every day—and that you never know where you'll go in them or what will happen—but you can control your dreams perfectly. That can't all be true, can it?"

Carol slid the bangles up and down her arm and tried to keep her temper. It was difficult to do when the sun was so hot and the noise coming from that pool so loud. She thought seriously of demoting Melville and making Chrestomanci into the villain in her next dream—until she remembered that there might not *be* a next dream unless Chrestomanci helped her. "I don't understand," she said.

"Let's talk about the dreams themselves then," said Chrestomanci. He pointed down the terrace steps to the blue, blue water of the pool. "There you see my ward, Janet. She's the fair-haired girl the others are just pushing off the diving board. She loves your dreams. She has all ninety-nine of them, though I am afraid Julia and the boys are very contemptuous about it. They say your dreams are slush and all exactly the same."

Naturally Carol was deeply hurt that anyone could call her dreams slush, but she knew better than to say so. She smiled graciously down at the large splash that was all she could see of Janet.

"Janet is hoping to meet you later," said Chrestomanci. Carol's smile broadened. She loved meeting admirers. "When I heard you were coming," Chrestomanci said, "I borrowed Janet's latest Omnibus Pillow." Carol's smile narrowed a bit. Chrestomanci did not seem the kind of person who would enjoy her dreams at all.

"I enjoyed it rather," Chrestomanci confessed. Carol's smile widened. Well! "But Julia and the boys are right, you know," Chrestomanci went on. "Your happy endings are pretty slushy, and the same sort of things happen in all of them." Carol's smile narrowed again distinctly at this. "But they're terribly lively," Chrestomanci said. "There's so much action and so many people. I like all those crowds—what your blurbs call your 'cast of thousands'—but I must confess I don't find your settings very convincing. That Arabian setting in the ninety-sixth dream was awful, even making allowances for how young you are. On the other hand, your fairground in the latest dream seemed to show the makings of a real gift."

By this time Carol's smile was going broad and narrow like the streets of Dublin's Fair City. She was almost caught off guard when Chrestomanci said, "And though you never appear in your dreams yourself, a number of characters do come in over and over again—in various disguises, of course. I make it about five or six main actors in all."

This was getting far too close to the things Carol never told even Mama. Luckily some reporters had made the same observation. "This is the way dreams are," she said. "And I am only the Seeing Eye."

"As you told the *Manchester Guardian*," Chrestomanci agreed, "if that is what they meant by 'Oosung Oyo.' I see that must have been a misprint now." He was looking very vague, to Carol's relief, and did not seem to notice her dismay. "Now," he said, "I suggest the time has come for you to go to sleep and let me see what happened to send your hundredth dream so wrong that you refused to record it."

"But nothing went wrong!" Carol protested. "I just didn't dream."

"So you say," said Chrestomanci. "Close your eyes. Feel free to snore if you wish."

"But—but I can't just go to sleep in the middle of a visit!" Carol said. "And—and those children in the pool are making far too much noise."

Chrestomanci put one hand casually down to the paving of the terrace. Carol saw his arm go up as if he were pulling something up out of the stones. The terrace went quiet. She could see the children splashing below, and their mouths opening and shutting, but not a sound came to her ears. "Have you run out of excuses now?" he asked.

"They're not excuses. And how are you going to know whether I dream or not without a proper dream spool and a qualified dream wizard to read it?" Carol demanded.

"Oh, I daresay I can manage quite well without," Chrestomanci remarked. Though he said it in a mild, sleepy sort of way, Carol suddenly remembered that he was a nine-lifed enchanter and more important than she was. She supposed he thought he was powerful enough on his own. Well, let him. She would humor him. Carol arranged her blue parasol to keep some of the sun off her and settled back in her deck chair, knowing nothing was going to happen . . .

. . . And she was at the fairground, where her ninety-ninth dream had left off. In front of her was a wide space of muddy grass, covered with bits of paper and other rubbish. She could see the Big Wheel in the distance behind some flapping tents and half-dismantled stalls and another tall thing that seemed to be most of the Helter-Skelter tower. The place seemed quite deserted.

"Well, *really!*" Carol said. "They still haven't cleared anything up! What are Martha and Paul *thinking* of?"

As soon as she said that, she clapped her hands guiltily to her mouth and whirled around to make sure that Chrestomanci had not come stalking up behind her. But there was nothing behind her but more dreary, litter-covered grass. Good! Carol thought. I *knew* nobody could come behind the scenes in a Carol Oneir private dream unless I let them! She relaxed. She was boss here. This was part of the things she never even told Mama, though, for a moment, back on the terrace at Teignes, she had been afraid that Chrestomanci was on to her.

The fact was, as Chrestomanci had noticed, Carol did only have six main characters working for her. There was Francis, tall and fair and handsome, with a beautiful baritone voice, who did all the heroes. He always ended up marrying the gentle but spirited Lucy, who was fair, too, and very pretty. Then there was Melville, who was thin and dark, with an evil white face, who did all the villains. Melville was so good at being a Baddie that Carol often used him several times in one dream. But he was always the gentleman, which was why polite Mr. Mindelbaum had reminded Carol of Melville.

The other three were Bimbo, who was oldish and who did all the Wise Old Men, Pathetic Cripples, and Weak Tyrants; Martha, who was the Older Woman and did the Aunts, Mothers, and Wicked Queens, either straight wicked or with Hearts of Gold; and Paul, who was small and boyish-looking. Paul's specialty was the Faithful Boy Assistant, though he did Second Baddie, too, and tended to get killed quite often in both kinds of parts. Paul and Martha, since they never had very big parts, were supposed to see that the cast of thousands cleared everything up between dreams.

Except that they hadn't this time.

"Paul!" Carol shouted. "Martha! Where's my cast of thousands?"

Nothing happened. Her voice just went rolling away into emptiness.

"Very well!" Carol called out. "I shall come and find you, and you won't like it when I do!"

She set off, picking her way disgustedly through the rubbish, toward those flapping tents. It really was too bad of them, she thought, to let her down like this, when she had gone to all the trouble of making them up and giving them a hundred disguises, and had made them as famous as she was herself, in a way. As Carol thought this, her bare foot came down in a melted ice cream. She jumped back with a shudder and found she was, for some reason, wearing a bathing suit like the children in Chrestomanci's pool.

"Oh, really!" she said crossly. She remembered now that her other attempt at a hundredth dream had gone like this, too, up to the point where she had scrapped it. Anyone would think this was the kind of dream ordinary people had. It wouldn't even make a decent Hatband dream. This time, with a sternly controlled effort, she made herself wear her blue button boots and the blue dress with all its petticoats underneath. It was hotter like that, but it showed that she was in charge. And she marched on, until she came to the flapping tents.

Here it nearly came like a common dream again. Carol walked up and down among empty tents and collapsed stalls, under the great framework of the Big Wheel and repeatedly past the topless Helter-Skelter tower, past roundabout after empty roundabout, without seeing a soul.

It was only her stern annoyance that kept her going until she did see someone, and then she nearly went straight past him, thinking he was one of the dummies from the Waxworks Show. He was sitting on a box beside a painted organ from a roundabout, staring. Perhaps some of the cast of thousands did work as dummies when necessary, Carol thought. She had no idea really. But this one was fair, so that meant he was a Goodie and generally worked with Francis.

"Hey, you!" she said. "Where's Francis?"

He gave her a dull, unfinished sort of look. "Rhubarb," he said. "Abracadabra."

"Yes, but you're not doing a crowd scene now," Carol told him. "I want to know where my Main Characters are."

The man pointed vaguely beyond the Big Wheel. "In their quarters," he said. "Committee meeting." So Carol set off that way. She had barely gone two steps when the man called out from behind her. "Hey, you! Say thank you!"

How rude! thought Carol. She turned and glared at him. He was now drinking out of a very strong-smelling green bottle. "You're drunk!" she said. "Where did you get that? I don't allow real drink in my dreams."

"Name's Norman," said the man. "Drowning sorrows."

Carol saw that she was not going to get any sense out of him. So she said, "Thank you," to stop him shouting after her again and went the way he had pointed. It led her among a huddle of gypsy caravans. Since these all had a blurred cardboard sort of look, Carol went straight past them, knowing they must belong to the cast of thousands. She knew the caravan she wanted would look properly clear and real. And it did. It was more like a tarry black shed on wheels than a caravan, but there was real black smoke pouring out of its rusty iron chimney.

Carol sniffed it. "Funny. It smells almost like toffee!" But she decided not to give her people any further warning. She marched up the black wooden ladder to the door and flung the door open.

Smoke and heat and the smell of drink and

toffee rolled out at her. Her people were all inside, but instead of turning politely to receive their orders as they usually did, none of them at first took any notice of her at all. Francis was sitting at the table playing cards with Martha, Paul, and Bimbo by the light of candles stuck in green bottles. Glasses of strong-smelling drink stood at each of their elbows, but most of the drink smell, to Carol's horror, was coming from the bottle Lucy was drinking out of. Beautiful, gentle Lucy was sitting on a bunk at the back, giggling and nursing a green bottle. As far as Carol could see in the poor light, Lucy's face looked like a gnome's, and her hair was what Mama would describe as "in tetters." Melville was cooking at the stove near the door. Carol was ashamed to look at him. He was wearing a grubby white apron and smiling a dreamy smile as he stirred his saucepan. Anything less villainous was hard to imagine.

"And just what," said Carol, "do you think you're all doing?"

At that, Francis turned around enough for her to see that he had not shaved for days. "Shut that blesh door, can' you!" he said irritably. It was possible he spoke that way because he had a large cigar between his teeth, but Carol feared it was more likely to be because Francis was drunk.

She shut the door and stood in front of it with her arms folded. "I want an explanation," she said. "I'm waiting."

Paul slapped down his cards and briskly pulled a pile of money toward himself. Then he took the cigar out of his boyish mouth to say, "And you can go on waiting, unless you've come to negotiate at last. We're on strike."

"On strike!" said Carol.

"On strike," Paul said. "All of us. I brought the cast of thousands out straight after the last dream. We want better working conditions and a bigger slice of the cake." He gave Carol a challenging and not very pleasant grin and put the cigar back in his mouth——a mouth that was not so boyish, now Carol looked at it closely. Paul was older than she had realized, with little cynical lines all over his face.

"Paul's our shop steward," Martha said. Martha, to Carol's surprise, was quite young, with reddish hair and a sulky, righteous look. Her voice had a bit of a whine to it when she went on. "We have our rights, you know. The conditions the cast of thousands have to live in are appalling, and it's one dream straight after another and no free time at all for any of us. And it's not as if we get job satisfaction either. The rotten parts Paul and I do!"

"Measly walk-ons," Paul said, busy dealing out cards. "One of the things we're protesting is being killed almost every dream. The cast of thousands gets gunned down in every final scene, and not only do they get no compensation, they have to get straight up and fight all through the next dream."

"'nd never allowsh ush any dthrink," Bimbo put in. Carol could see he was very drunk. His nose was purple with it, and his white hair looked damp. "Got shick of colored water. Had to shteal fruit from Enshanted Garden dream to make firsht wine. Make whishky now. It'sh better."

"It's not as if you *paid* us anything," Martha whined. "We have to take what reward we can get for our services."

"Then where did you get all that money?" Carol demanded, pointing to the large heap in front of Paul.

"The Arabian treasure scene and so forth," said Paul. "Pirates' hoard. Most of it's only painted paper."

Francis suddenly said, in a loud, slurry voice,

"I want recognition. I've been ninety-nine differ-ent heroes, but not a word of credit goes on any pillow or jar." He banged the table. "Exploitation! That's what it is!"

"Yes, we all want our names on the next dream," Paul said. "Melville, give her our list of complaints, will you?"

"Melville's our Strike Committee secretary," said Martha.

Francis banged the table again and shouted, *"Melville!"* Then everyone else shouted, "MEL-VILLE!" until Melville finally turned around from the stove holding his saucepan in one hand and a sheet of paper in the other.

"I didn't want to spoil my fudge," Melville said apologetically. He handed the paper to Carol. "There, my dear. This wasn't my idea, but I didn't wish to let the others down."

Carol, by this time, was backed against the door, more or less in tears. This dream seemed to be a nightmare. "Lucy!" she called out desperately. "Lucy, are you in this, too?"

"Don't you disturb her," said Martha, whom Carol was beginning to dislike very much. "Lucy's suffered enough. She's had her fill of parts that make her a plaything and property of men.

Haven't you, love?" she called to Lucy.

Lucy looked up. "Nobody understands," she said, staring mournfully at the wall. "I hate Francis. And I always have to marry him and live hap-*hic*-hallipy ever after."

This, not surprisingly, annoyed Francis. "And I hate *you*!" he bawled, jumping up as he shouted. The table went over with a crash, and the glasses, money, cards, and candles went with it. In the terrifying dark scramble that followed, the door somehow burst open behind Carol, and she got herself out through it as fast as she could . . .

. . . And found herself sitting on a deck chair on the sunny terrace again. She was holding a paper in one hand, and her parasol was rolling by her feet. To her annoyance, someone had spilled a long, sticky trickle of what seemed to be fudge all down her blue dress.

"*Tonino! Vieni qui!*" somebody called.

Carol looked up to find Chrestomanci trying to put together a broken deck chair in the midst of a crowd of people who were all pushing past him and hurrying away down the terrace steps. Carol could not think who the people were at first, until she caught a glimpse of Francis among them, and then Lucy, who had one hand clutched around her bottle and the other in the hand of Norman, the man Carol had first met sitting on a box. The rest of them must be the cast of thousands, she supposed. She was still trying to imagine what had happened when Chrestomanci dropped the broken deck chair and stopped the very last person to cross the terrace.

"Excuse me, sir," Chrestomanci said. "Would you mind explaining a few things before you leave?"

It was Melville, still in his cook's apron, waving smoke away from his saucepan with one long, villainous hand and peering down at his fudge with a very doleful look on his long, villainous face. "I think it's spoiled," he said. "You want to know what happened? Well, I think the cast of thousands started it, around the time Lucy fell in love with Norman, so it may have been Norman's doing to begin with. Anyway, they began complaining that they never got a chance to be real people, and Paul heard them. Paul is very ambitious, you know, and he knew, as we all did, that Francis isn't really cut out to be a hero—"

"No, indeed. He has a weak chin," Chrestomanci agreed.

Carol gasped and was just about to make a

protest—which would have been a rather tearful one at that moment—when she recalled that Francis's bristly chin had indeed looked rather small and wobbly under that cigar.

"Oh, you shouldn't judge by chins," said Melville. "Look at mine—and I'm no more a villain than Francis is a hero. But Francis has his petulant side, and Paul played on that, with the help of Bimbo and his whisky, and Lucy was with Paul anyway because she hated being forced to wear frilly dresses and simper at Francis. She and Norman want to take up farming. And Martha, who is a very frivolous girl to my mind, came in with them because she cannot abide having to clear up the scenery at such short notice. So then they all came to me."

"And you held out?" asked Chrestomanci.

"All through *The Cripple of Monte Christo* and *The Arabian Knight*," Melville admitted, ambling across the terrace to park his saucepan on the balustrade. "I am fond of Carol, you see, and I am quite ready to be three villains at once for her if that is what she wants. But when she started on the Fairground dream straight after *The Tyrant of London Town*, I had to admit that we were all being thoroughly overworked. None of us got any time to be ourselves.

Dear me," he added. "I think the cast of thousands is preparing to paint the town red."

Chrestomanci came and leaned on the balustrade to see. "I fear so," he said. "What do you think makes Carol work you all so hard? Ambition?"

There was now such a noise coming from the town that Carol could not resist getting up to look, too. Large numbers of the cast of thousands had made straight for the beach. They were joyously racing into the water, pulling little wheeled bathing huts after them, or simply casting their clothes away and plunging in. This was causing quite an outcry from the regular holidaymakers. More outcries came from the main square below the casino, where the cast of thousands had flooded into all the elegant cafés, shouting for ice cream, wine, and frogs' legs.

"It looks rather fun," said Melville. "No, not ambition exactly, sir. Say rather that Carol was caught up in success, and her mama was caught up with her. It is not easy to stop something when one's mama expects one to go on and on."

A horse-drawn cab was now galloping along the main street, pursued by shouting, scrambling, excited people. Pursuing these was a little posse of gendarmes. This seemed to be because the white-bearded person in the cab was throwing handfuls of jewels in all directions in the most abandoned way. Arabian jewels and pirates' treasure mostly, Carol thought. She wondered if they would turn out to be glass or real jewels.

"Poor Bimbo," said Melville. "He sees himself as a sort of kingly Santa Claus these days. He has played those parts too often. I think he should retire."

"And what a pity your mama told your cab to wait," Chrestomanci said to Carol. "Isn't that Francis, Martha, and Paul there? Just going into the casino."

They were, too. Carol saw them waltzing arm in arm up the marble steps, three people obviously going on a spree.

"Paul," said Melville, "tells me he has a system to break the bank."

"A fairly common delusion," said Chrestomanci.

"But he can't!" said Carol. "He hasn't got any real money!" She chanced to look down as she spoke. Her diamond pendant was gone. So was her diamond brooch. Her sapphire bangles and every one of her gold ones were missing. Even the clasps of her handbag had been torn off. "They robbed me!" she cried out.

"That would be Martha," Melville said sadly. "Remember she picked pockets in *The Tyrant of London Town*."

"It sounds as if you owed them quite a sum in wages," Chrestomanci said.

"But what shall I *do*?" Carol wailed. "How am I going to get everyone back?"

Melville looked worried for her. It came out as a villainous grimace, but Carol understood perfectly. Melville was sweet.

Chrestomanci just looked surprised and a little bored. "You mean you *want* all these people back?" he said.

Carol opened her mouth to say yes, of course she did! But she did not say it. They were having such fun. Bimbo was having the time of his life, galloping through the streets, throwing jewels. The people in the sea were a happy, splashing mass, and waiters were hurrying about down in the square, taking orders and slapping down plates and glasses in front of the cast of thousands in the cafés. Carol just hoped they were using real money. If she turned her head, she could see that some of the cast of thousands had now got as far as the golf course, where most of them seemed to be under the impression that golf was a team game that you played rather like hockey.

"While Carol makes up her mind," said Chrestomanci, "what, Melville, is your personal opinion of her dreams? As one who has an inside view?"

Melville pulled his mustache unhappily. "I was afraid you were going to ask me that," he said. "She has tremendous talent, of course, or she couldn't do it at all, but I do sometimes feel that she—well—she repeats herself. Put it like this: I think maybe Carol doesn't give herself a chance to be herself any more than she gives us."

Melville, Carol realized, was the only one of her people she really liked. She was heartily sick of all the others. Though she had not admitted it, they had bored her for years, but she had never had time to think of anyone more interesting because she had always been so busy getting on with the next dream. Suppose she gave them all the sack? But wouldn't that hurt Melville's feelings?

"Melville," she said anxiously, "do you enjoy being villains?"

"My dear," said Melville, "it's up to you entirely, but I confess that sometimes I would like to try being someone . . . well . . . not black-hearted. Say, *gray*-hearted, and a little more complicated."

This was difficult. "If I did that," Carol said, thinking about it, "I'd have to stop dreaming for a while and spend a time—maybe a long time—sort of getting a new outlook on people. Would you mind waiting? It might take over a year."

"Not at all," said Melville. "Just call me when you need me." And he bent over and kissed Carol's hand, in his best and most villainous manner . . .

. . . And Carol was once again sitting up in her deck chair. This time, however, she was rubbing her eyes, and the terrace was empty except for Chrestomanci, holding a broken deck chair, and talking in what seemed to be Italian to a skinny little boy. The boy seemed to have come up from the bathing pool. He was wearing bathing trunks and dripping water all over the paving.

"Oh!" said Carol. "So it was only a dream really!" She noticed she must have dropped her parasol while she was asleep and reached to pick it up. Someone seemed to have trodden on it. And there was a long trickle of fudge on her dress. Then of course she looked for her brooch, her pendant, and her bangles. They were gone. Someone had torn her dress pulling the brooch off. Her eyes leaped to the balustrade and found a small burned saucepan standing on it.

At that, Carol jumped and ran to the balustrade, hoping to see Melville on his way down the stairs from the terrace. The stairs were empty. But she was in time to see Bimbo's cab, surrounded by gendarmes and stopped at the end of the parade. Bimbo did not seem to be in it. It looked as if he had worked the disappearing act she had invented for him in *The Cripple of Monte Christo*.

Down on the beach, crowds of the cast of thousands were coming out of the sea and lying down to sunbathe, or politely borrowing beach balls from the other holidaymakers. She could hardly tell them from the regular tourists, in fact. Out on the golf links, the cast of thousands there was being sorted out by a man in a red blazer and lined up to practice tee shots. Carol looked at the casino then, but there was no sign of Paul or Martha or Francis. Around the square, however, there was singing coming from the crowded cafés—steady, swelling singing, for of course there were several massed choirs among the cast of thousands. Carol turned and looked accusingly at Chrestomanci.

Chrestomanci broke off his Italian conversation in order to bring the small boy over by one wet, skinny shoulder. "Tonino here," he said, "is a rather unusual magician. He reinforces other people's magic. When I saw the way your thoughts were going, I thought we'd better have him up to back up your decision. I suspected you might do something like this. That's why I didn't want any reporters. Wouldn't you like to come down to the pool now? I'm sure Janet can lend you a swimsuit and probably a clean dress as well."

"Well . . . thank you . . . yes, please . . . but . . ." Carol began, when the small boy pointed to something behind her.

"I speak English," he said. "You dropped your paper."

Carol dived around and picked it up. In beautiful sloping writing, it said:

Carol Oneir hereby releases Francis, Lucy, Martha, Paul, and Bimbo from all further professional duties and gives the cast of thousands leave of indefinite absence. I am taking a holiday with your kind permission, and I remain Your servant,
Melville

"Oh, good!" said Carol. "Oh, dear! What shall I do about Mr. Ploys? And how shall I break it to Mama?"

"I can speak to Ploys," said Chrestomanci, "but your mama is strictly your problem, though your father, when he gets back from the casin—er, fishing—will certainly back you up."

Dad did back Carol up some hours later, and Mama was slightly easier to deal with than usual anyway, because she was so confused at the way she had mistaken Chrestomanci's wife for a servant. By that time, however, the main thing Carol wanted to tell Dad was that she had been pushed off the diving board sixteen times and had learned to swim two strokes—well, almost.

THE SAGE OF THEARE

T HERE WAS A WORLD called Theare in
which Heaven was very well organized.
Everything was so precisely worked out
that every god knew his or her exact duties, correct prayers, right times for business, utterly exact
character, and unmistakable place above or below
the gods.

This was the case from Great Zond, the king
of the gods, through every god, godlet, deity,
minor deity, and numen, down to the most imma-
terial nymph. Even the invisible dragons that lived
in the rivers had their invisible lines of demarca-
tion. The universe ran like clockwork. Mankind
was not always so regular, but the gods were there
to set him right. It had been like this for centuries.

So it was a breach in the very nature of things
when, in the middle of the yearly Festival of

Water, at which only watery deities were entitled to be present, Great Zond looked up to see Imperion, god of the sun, storming toward him down the halls of Heaven.

"Go away!" cried Zond, aghast.

But Imperion swept on, causing the watery deities gathered there to steam and hiss, and arrived in a wave of heat and warm water at the foot of Zond's high throne.

"Father!" Imperion cried urgently.

A high god like Imperion was entitled to call Zond Father. Zond did not recall whether or not he was actually Imperion's father. The origins of the gods were not quite so orderly as their present existence. But Zond knew that, son of his or not, Imperion had breached all the rules. "Abase yourself," Zond said sternly.

Imperion ignored this command, too. Perhaps this was just as well, since the floor of Heaven was awash already, and steaming. Imperion kept his flaming gaze on Zond. "Father! The Sage of Dissolution has been born!"

Zond shuddered in the clouds of hot vapor and tried to feel resigned. "It is written," he said, "a Sage shall be born who shall question everything. His questions shall bring down the exquisite order of Heaven and cast all the gods into disorder. It is also written—"

Here Zond realized that Imperion had made him break the rules, too. The correct procedure was for Zond to summon the god of prophecy and have that god consult the Book of Heaven. Then he realized that Imperion *was* the god of prophecy. It was one of his precisely allocated duties. Zond rounded on Imperion. "What do you mean coming and telling me? You're god of prophecy! Go and look in the Book of Heaven!"

"I already have, Father," said Imperion. "I find I prophesied the coming of the Sage of Dissolution when the gods first began. It is written that the Sage shall be born and that I shall not know."

"Then," said Zond, scoring a point, "how is it you're here telling me he *has* been born?"

"The mere fact," Imperion said, "that I can come here and interrupt the Water Festival shows that the Sage has been born. Our Dissolution has obviously begun."

There was a splash of consternation among the watery gods. They were gathered down the hall as far as they could get from Imperion, but they had all heard. Zond tried to gather his wits. What with the steam raised by Imperion and the spume of dismay thrown out by the rest, the halls of Heaven were in a state nearer chaos than he had known for millennia. Any more of this, and there would be no need for the Sage to ask questions.

"Leave us," Zond said to the watery gods. "Events even beyond my control cause this festival to be stopped. You will be informed later of any decision I make." To Zond's dismay, the watery ones hesitated—further evidence of Dissolution. "I promise," he said.

The watery ones made up their minds. They left in waves, all except one. This one was Ock, god of all oceans. Ock was equal in status to Imperion, and heat did not threaten him. He stayed where he was.

Zond was not pleased. Ock, it always seemed to him, was the least orderly of the gods. He did not know his place. He was as restless and unfathomable as mankind. But, with Dissolution already begun, what could Zond do?

"You have our permission to stay," he said graciously to Ock, and to Imperion: "Well, how did you know the Sage was born?"

"I was consulting the Book of Heaven on another matter," said Imperion, "and the page opened at my prophecy concerning the Sage of Dissolution. Since it said that I would not know the day and hour when the Sage was born, it followed that he has already been born, or I would not have known. The rest of the prophecy was commendably precise, however. Twenty years from now, he will start questioning Heaven. What shall we do to stop him?"

"I don't see what we can do," Zond said hopelessly. "A prophecy is a prophecy."

"But we must do something!" blazed Imperion. "I insist! I am a god of order, even more than you are. Think what would happen if the sun went inaccurate! This means more to me than anyone. I want the Sage of Dissolution found and killed before he can ask questions."

Zond was shocked. "I can't do that! If the prophecy says he has to ask questions, then he has to ask them."

Here Ock approached. "Every prophecy has a loophole," he said.

"Of course," snapped Imperion. "I can see the loophole as well as you. I'm taking advantage of the disorder caused by the birth of the Sage to ask Great Zond to kill him and overthrow the prophecy. Thus restoring order."

"Logic chopping is not what I meant," said Ock.

The two gods faced one another. Steam from Ock suffused Imperion and then rained back on Ock, as regularly as breathing. "What *did* you mean, then?" said Imperion.

"The prophecy," said Ock, "does not appear to say which world the Sage will ask his questions in. There are many other worlds. Mankind calls them if-worlds, meaning that they were once the same world as Theare, but split off and went their own ways after each doubtful event in history. Each if-world has its own Heaven. There must be one world in which the gods are not as orderly as we are here. Let the Sage be put in that world. Let him ask his predestined questions there."

"Good idea!" Zond clapped his hands in relief, causing untoward tempests in all Theare. "Agreed, Imperion?"

"Yes," said Imperion. He flamed with relief. And being unguarded, he at once became prophetic. "But I must warn you," he said, "that strange things happen when destiny is tampered with."

"Strange things maybe, but never disorderly," Zond asserted. He called the water gods back and, with them, every god in Theare. He told them that an infant had just been born who was destined to spread Dissolution, and he ordered each one of them to search the ends of the earth for this child.

("The ends of the earth" was a legal formula. Zond did not believe that Theare was flat. But the expression had been unchanged for centuries, just like the rest of Heaven. It meant "Look everywhere.")

The whole of Heaven looked high and low. Nymphs and godlets scanned mountains, caves, and woods. Household gods peered into cradles. Watery gods searched beaches, banks, and margins. The goddess of love went deeply into her records, to find who the Sage's parents might be. The invisible dragons swam to look inside barges and houseboats. Since there was a god for everything in Theare, nowhere was missed, nothing was omitted. Imperion searched harder than any, blazing into every nook and crevice on one side of the world, and exhorting the moon goddess to do the same on the other side.

And nobody found the Sage. There were one or two false alarms, such as when a household goddess reported an infant that never stopped crying. This baby, she said, was driving her up the wall and, if this was not Dissolution, she would like to know what was. There were also several reports of infants born with teeth, or six fingers, or suchlike strangeness. But in each case Zond was able to prove that the child had nothing to do with Dissolution. After a month it became clear that the infant Sage was not going to be found.

Imperion was in despair, for as he had told Zond, order meant more to him than to any other god. He became so worried that he was actually causing the sun to lose heat. At length the goddess of love advised him to go off and relax with a mortal woman before he brought about Dissolution himself.

Imperion saw she was right. He went down to visit the human woman he had loved for some years. It was established custom for gods to love mortals. Some visited their loves in all sorts of fanciful shapes, and some had many loves at once. But Imperion was both honest and faithful. He never visited Nestara as anything but a handsome man, and he loved her devotedly. Three years ago she had borne him a son, whom Imperion loved almost as much as he loved Nestara. Before the Sage was born to trouble him, Imperion had been trying to bend the rules of Heaven a little, to get his son approved as a god, too.

The child's name was Thasper. As Imperion descended to earth, he could see Thasper digging in some sand outside Nestara's house—a beautiful child, fair-haired and blue-eyed. Imperion wondered fondly if Thasper was talking properly yet. Nestara had been worried about how slow he was learning to speak.

Imperion alighted beside his son. "Hello, Thasper. What are you digging so busily?"

Instead of answering, Thasper raised his golden head and shouted. "Mum!" he yelled. "Why does it go so bright when Dad comes?"

All Imperion's pleasure vanished. Of course no one could ask questions until he had learned to speak. But it would be too cruel if his own son turned out to be the Sage of Dissolution. "Why shouldn't it go bright?" he asked defensively.

Thasper scowled up at him. "I want to know. *Why* does it?"

"Perhaps because you feel happy to see me," Imperion suggested.

"I'm not happy," Thasper said. His lower lip came out. Tears filled his big blue eyes. "Why does it go bright? I want to know. Mum! I'm not happy!"

Nestara came racing out of the house, almost too concerned to smile at Imperion. "Thasper love, what's the matter?"

"I want to *know!*" wailed Thasper.

"What do you want to know? I've never known such an inquiring mind," Nestara said proudly to Imperion, as she picked Thasper up. "That's why he was so slow talking. He wouldn't speak until he'd found out how to ask questions. And if you don't give him an exact answer, he'll cry for hours."

"When did he first start asking questions?" Imperion inquired tensely.

"About a month ago," said Nestara.

This made Imperion truly miserable, but he concealed it. It was clear to him that Thasper was indeed the Sage of Dissolution and he was going to have to take him away to another world. He smiled and said, "My love, I have wonderful news for you. Thasper has been accepted as a god. Great Zond himself will have him as cupbearer."

"Oh, not now!" cried Nestara. "He's so little!"

She made numerous other objections, too. But, in the end she let Imperion take Thasper. After all, what better future could there be for a child? She put Thasper into Imperion's arms with all sorts of anxious advice about what he ate and when he went to bed. Imperion kissed her good-bye, heavyhearted. He was not a god of deception. He knew he dared not see her again for fear he told her the truth.

Then, with Thasper in his arms, Imperion went up to the middle regions below Heaven, to look for another world.

Thasper looked down with interest at the great blue curve of the world. "Why—" he began.

Imperion hastily enclosed him in a sphere of forgetfulness. He could not afford to let Thasper ask things here. Questions that spread Dissolution on earth would have an even more powerful effect in the middle region. The sphere was a silver globe, neither transparent nor opaque. In it, Thasper would stay seemingly asleep, not moving and not growing, until the sphere was opened. With the child thus safe, Imperion hung the sphere from one shoulder and stepped into the next-door world.

He went from world to world. He was pleased to find there were an almost infinite number of them, for the choice proved supremely difficult. Some worlds were so disorderly that he shrank from leaving Thasper in them. In some, the gods resented Imperion's intrusion and shouted at him to be off. In others, it was mankind that was resentful. One world he came to was so rational that, to his horror, he found the gods were dead. There were many others he thought might do, until he let the spirit of prophecy blow through him, and in each case this told him that harm would come to Thasper here.

But at last he found a good world. It seemed calm and elegant. The few gods there seemed civilized but casual. Indeed, Imperion was a little puzzled to find that these gods seemed to share quite a lot of their power with mankind. But mankind did not seem to abuse this power, and the spirit of prophecy assured him that if he left Thasper here inside his sphere of forgetfulness, it would be opened by someone who would treat the boy well.

Imperion put the sphere down in a wood and sped back to Theare, heartily relieved. There he reported what he had done to Zond, and all Heaven rejoiced. Imperion made sure that Nestara married a very rich man who gave her not only wealth and happiness but plenty of children to replace Thasper. Then, a little sadly, he went back to the ordered life of Heaven. The exquisite organization of Theare went on untroubled by Dissolution.

Seven years passed.

All that while Thasper knew nothing and remained three years old. Then, one day, the sphere of forgetfulness fell in two halves, and he blinked in sunlight somewhat less golden than he had known.

"So that's what was causing all the disturbance," a tall man murmured.

"Poor little soul," said a lady.

There was a wood around Thasper, and people standing in it looking at him, but, as far as Thasper knew, nothing had happened since he soared to the middle region with his father. He went on with the question he had been in the middle of asking. "Why is the world round?" he said.

"Interesting question," said the tall man. "The answer usually given is because the corners wore off spinning around the sun. But it could be designed to make us end where we began."

"Sir, you'll muddle him, talking like that," said another lady. "He's only little."

"No, he's interested," said another man. "Look at him."

Thasper was indeed interested. He approved

of the tall man. He was a little puzzled about where he had come from, but he supposed the tall man must have been put there because he answered questions better than Imperion. He wondered where Imperion had got to. "Why aren't you my dad?" he asked the tall man.

"Another most penetrating question," said the tall man. "Because, as far as we can find out, your father lives in another world. Tell me your name."

This was another point in the tall man's favor. Thasper never answered questions; he only asked them. But this was a command. The tall man understood Thasper.

"Thasper," Thasper answered obediently.

"He's sweet!" said the first lady. "I want to adopt him." To which the other ladies gathered around most heartily agreed.

"Impossible," said the tall man. His tone was mild as milk and rock firm. The ladies were reduced to begging to be able to look after Thasper for a day, then. An hour. "No," the tall man said mildly. "He must go back at once." At which all the ladies cried out that Thasper might be in great danger in his own home. The tall man said, "I shall take care of that, of course." Then he stretched out a hand and pulled Thasper up.

"Come along, Thasper."

As soon as Thasper was out of it, the two halves of the sphere vanished. One of the ladies took his other hand and he was led away, first on a jiggly ride, which he much enjoyed, and then into a huge house, where there was a very perplexing room. In this room, Thasper sat in a five-pointed star and pictures kept appearing around him. People kept shaking their heads. "No, not that world either." The tall man answered all Thasper's questions, and Thasper was too interested even to be annoyed when they would not allow him anything to eat.

"Why not?" he said.

"Because just by being here, you are causing the world to jolt about," the tall man explained. "If you put food inside you, food is a heavy part of this world, and it might jolt you to pieces."

Soon after that a new picture appeared. Everyone said, "Ah!" and the tall man said, "So it's Theare!" He looked at Thasper in a surprised way. "You must have struck someone as disorderly," he said. Then he looked at the picture again, in a lazy, careful kind of way. "No disorder," he said. "No danger. Come with me."

He took Thasper's hand again and led him

into the picture. As he did so, Thasper's hair turned much darker. "A simple precaution," the tall man murmured, a little apologetically, but Thasper did not even notice. He was not aware what color his hair had been to start with, and besides, he was taken up with surprise at how fast they were going. They whizzed into a city and stopped abruptly. It was a good house, just on the edge of a poorer district. "Here is someone who will do," the tall man said, and he knocked at the door.

A sad-looking lady opened the door.

"I beg your pardon, madam," said the tall man. "Have you by any chance lost a small boy?"

"Yes," said the lady. "But this isn't—" She blinked, "Yes, it *is!*" she cried out. "Oh, Thasper! How could you run off like that? Thank you so much, sir." But the tall man had gone.

The lady's name was Alina Altun, and she was so convinced that she was Thasper's mother that Thasper was soon convinced, too. He settled in happily with her and her husband, who was a doctor, hard working but not very rich.

Thasper soon forgot the tall man, Imperion, and Nestara. Sometimes it did puzzle him—and his new mother, too—that when she showed him off to her friends, she always felt bound to say, "This is Badien, but we always call him Thasper." Thanks to the tall man, none of them ever knew that the real Badien had wandered away the day Thasper came, and fallen in the river, where an invisible dragon ate him.

If Thasper had remembered the tall man, he might also have wondered why his arrival seemed to start Dr. Altun on the road to prosperity. The people in the poorer district nearby suddenly discovered what a good doctor Dr. Altun was, and how little he charged. Alina was shortly able to afford to send Thasper to a very good school, where Thasper often exasperated his teachers by his many questions. He had, as his new mother often proudly said, a most inquiring mind. Although he learned quicker than most the Ten First Lessons and the Nine Graces of Childhood, his teachers were nonetheless often annoyed enough to snap, "Oh, go and ask an invisible dragon!" which is what people in Theare often said when they thought they were being pestered.

Thasper did, with difficulty, gradually cure himself of his habit of never answering questions. But he always preferred asking to answering. At home he asked questions all the time: "Why does the kitchen god go and report to Heaven once a year? Is it so I can steal biscuits? Why are there invisible dragons? Is there a god for everything? Why is there a god for everything? If the gods make people ill, how can Dad cure them? Why must I have a baby brother or sister?"

Alina Altun was a good mother. She most diligently answered all these questions, including the last. She told Thasper how babies were made, ending her account with "Then, if the gods bless my womb, a baby will come." She was a devout person.

"I don't want you to be blessed!" Thasper said, resorting to a statement, which he only did when he was strongly moved.

He seemed to have no choice in the matter. By the time he was ten years old, the gods had thought fit to bless him with two brothers and two sisters. In Thasper's opinion, they were, as blessings, very low grade. They were just too young to be any use. "Why can't they be the same age as me?" he demanded many times. He began to bear the gods a small but definite grudge about this.

Dr. Altun continued to prosper, and his earnings more than kept pace with his family. Alina employed a nursemaid, a cook, and a number of rather impermanent houseboys. It was one of these houseboys who, when Thasper was eleven, shyly presented Thasper with a folded square of paper. Wondering, Thasper unfolded it. It gave him a curious feeling to touch, as if the paper was vibrating a little in his fingers. It also gave out a very strong warning that he was not to mention it to anybody. It said:

> Dear Thasper,
> Your situation is an odd one. Make sure
> that you call me at the moment when
> you come face-to-face with yourself. I
> shall be watching and I will come at once.
> Yrs,
> *Chrestomanci*

Since Thasper by now had not the slightest recollection of his early life, this letter puzzled him extremely. He knew he was not supposed to tell anyone about it, but he also knew that this did not include the houseboy. With the letter in his hand, he hurried after the houseboy to the kitchen.

He was stopped at the head of the kitchen

stairs by a tremendous smashing of china from below. This was followed immediately by the cook's voice raised in nonstop abuse. Thasper knew it was no good trying to go into the kitchen.

The houseboy—who went by the odd name of Cat—was in the process of getting fired, like all the other houseboys before him. He had better go and wait for Cat outside the back door. Thasper looked at the letter in his hand. As he did so, his fingers tingled. The letter vanished.

"It's gone!" he exclaimed, showing by this statement how astonished he was. He never could account for what he did next. Instead of going to wait for the houseboy, he ran to the living room, intending to tell his mother about it, in spite of the warning.

"Do you know what?" he began. He had invented this meaningless question so that he could tell people things and still make it into an inquiry. "Do you know what?" Alina looked up. Thasper, though he fully intended to tell her about the mysterious letter, found himself saying, "The cook's just sacked the new houseboy."

"Oh, bother!" said Alina. "I shall have to find another one now."

Annoyed with himself, Thasper tried to tell

her again. "Do you know what? I'm surprised the cook doesn't sack the kitchen god, too."

"Hush, dear. Don't talk about the gods that way!" said the devout lady.

By this time the houseboy had left, and Thasper lost the urge to tell anyone about the letter. It remained with him as his own personal exciting secret. He thought of it as the Letter from a Person Unknown. He sometimes whispered the strange name of the Person Unknown to himself when no one could hear. But nothing ever happened, even when he said the name out loud. He gave up doing that after a while. He had other things to think about. He became fascinated by Rules, Laws, and Systems.

Rules and Systems were an important part of the life of mankind in Theare. It stood to reason, with Heaven so well organized. People codified all behavior into things like the Seven Subtle Politenesses or the Hundred Roads to Godliness. Thasper had been taught these things from the time he was three years old.

He was accustomed to hearing Alina argue the niceties of the Seventy-two Household Laws with her friends. Now Thasper suddenly discovered for himself that all Rules made a magnificent framework for one's mind to clamber about in. He made lists of rules, and refinements on rules, and possible ways of doing the opposite of what the rules said while still keeping the rules. He invented new codes of rules. He filled books and made charts. He invented games with huge and complicated rules and played them with his friends.

Onlookers found these games both rough and muddled, but Thasper and his friends reveled in them. The best moment in any game was when somebody stopped playing and shouted, "I've thought of a new rule!"

This obsession with rules lasted until Thasper was fifteen. He was walking home from school one day, thinking over a list of rules for Twenty Fashionable Hairstyles. From this it will be seen that Thasper was noticing girls, though none of the girls had so far seemed to notice him. And he was thinking which girl should wear which hairstyle when his attention was caught by words chalked on the wall:

IF RULES MAKE A FRAMEWORK FOR
THE MIND TO CLIMB ABOUT IN,
WHY SHOULD THE MIND NOT CLIMB

RIGHT OUT?
SAYS THE SAGE OF DISSOLUTION

That same day there was consternation again in Heaven. Zond summoned all the high gods to his throne. "The Sage of Dissolution has started to preach," he announced direfully. "Imperion, I thought you got rid of him."

"I thought I did," Imperion said. He was even more appalled than Zond. If the Sage had started to preach, it meant that Imperion had got rid of Thasper and deprived himself of Nestara quite unnecessarily. "I must have been mistaken," he admitted.

Here Ock spoke up, steaming gently. "Father Zond," he said, "may I respectfully suggest that you deal with the Sage yourself, so that there will be no mistake this time?"

"That was just what I was about to suggest," Zond said gratefully. "Are you all agreed?"

All the gods agreed. They were too used to order to do otherwise.

As for Thasper, he was staring at the chalked words, shivering to the soles of his sandals. What was this? Who was using his own private thoughts about rules? Who was this Sage of Dissolution?

Thasper was ashamed. He, who was so good at asking questions, had never thought of asking this one. Why should one's mind not climb right out of the rules after all?

He went home and asked his parents about the Sage of Dissolution. He fully expected them to know. He was quite agitated when they did not. But they had a neighbor, who sent Thasper to another neighbor, who had a friend, who, when Thasper finally found his house, said he had heard that the Sage was a clever young man who made a living by mocking the gods.

The next day someone had washed the words off. But the day after that a badly printed poster appeared on the same wall.

THE SAGE OF DISSOLUTION ASKS
BY WHOSE ORDER IS ORDER
ANYWAY??
COME TO SMALL UNCTION
SUBLIME CONCERT HALL
TONIGHT 6:30

At 6:20 Thasper was having supper. At 6:24 he made up his mind and left the table. At 6:32 he arrived panting at Small Unction Hall. It proved to be a small shabby building quite near where he lived. Nobody was there. As far as Thasper could gather from the grumpy caretaker, the meeting had been the night before. Thasper turned away, deeply disappointed. Who ordered the order was a question he now longed to know the answer to. It was deep. He had a notion that the man who called himself the Sage of Dissolution was truly brilliant.

By way of feeding his own disappointment, he went to school the next day by a route which took him past the Small Unction Concert Hall. It had burned down in the night. There were only blackened brick walls left. When he got to school, a number of people were talking about it. They said it had burst into flames just before seven the night before.

"Did you know," Thasper said, "that the Sage of Dissolution was there the day before yesterday?"

That was how he discovered he was not the only one interested in the Sage. Half his class were admirers of Dissolution. That, too, was when the girls deigned to notice him. "He's amazing about the gods," one girl told him. "No one ever asked questions like that before."

Most of the class, however, girls and boys alike, only knew a little more than Thasper, and most of what they knew was secondhand. But a boy showed him a carefully cut-out newspaper article in which a well-known scholar discussed what he called "the so-called Doctrine of Dissolution." It said, long-windedly, that the Sage and his followers were rude to the gods and against all the rules.

It did not tell Thasper much, but it was something. He saw, rather ruefully, that his obsession with rules had been quite wrongheaded and had, into the bargain, caused him to fall behind the rest of his class in learning of this wonderful new doctrine. He became a Disciple of Dissolution on the spot. He joined the rest of his class in finding out all they could about the Sage.

He went around with them, writing up on walls:

DISSOLUTION RULES OK.

For a long while after that, the only thing any of Thasper's class could learn of the Sage were scraps of questions chalked on walls and quickly rubbed out.

WHAT NEED OF PRAYER?

WHY SHOULD THERE BE A HUNDRED
ROADS TO GODLINESS, NOT MORE
OR LESS?

DO WE CLIMB ANYWHERE ON THE
STEPS TO HEAVEN?

WHAT IS PERFECTION: A PROCESS
OR A STATE?

WHEN WE CLIMB TO PERFECTION, IS
THIS A MATTER FOR THE GODS?

Thasper obsessively wrote all these sayings
down. He was obsessed again, he admitted, but
this time it was in a new way. He was thinking,
thinking. At first he thought simply of clever
questions to ask the Sage. He strained to find
questions no one had asked before. But in the
process his mind seemed to loosen, and shortly he
was thinking of how the Sage might answer his
questions. He considered order and rules and
Heaven, and it came to him that there was a
reason behind all the brilliant questions the Sage
asked. He felt light-headed with thinking.

The reason behind the Sage's questions came to him the morning he was shaving for the first time. He thought, The gods need human beings in order to be gods! Blinded with this revelation, Thasper stared into the mirror at his own face half covered with white foam. Without humans believing in them, gods were nothing! The order of Heaven, the rules and codes of earth, were all only there because of people! It was transcendent.

As Thasper stared, the Letter from the Unknown came into his mind. "Is this being face-to-face with myself?" he said. But he was not sure. And he became sure that when that time came, he would not have to wonder.

Then it came to him that the Unknown Chrestomanci was almost certainly the Sage himself. He was thrilled. The Sage was taking a special mysterious interest in one teenage boy, Thasper Altun. The vanishing letter exactly fitted the elusive Sage.

The Sage continued elusive. The next firm news of him was a newspaper report of the Celestial Gallery's being struck by lightning. The roof of the building collapsed, said the report, "only seconds after the young man known as the Sage of Dissolution had delivered another of his anguished and self-doubting homilies and left the building with his disciples."

"He's not self-doubting," Thasper said to himself. "He knows about the gods. If *I* know, then *he* certainly does."

He and his classmates went on a pilgrimage to the ruined gallery. It was a better building than Small Unction Hall. It seemed the Sage was going up in the world.

Then there was enormous excitement. One of the girls found a small advertisement in a paper. The Sage was to deliver another lecture, in the huge Kingdom of Splendor Hall. He had gone up in the world again. Thasper and his friends dressed in their best and went there in a body. But it seemed as if the time for the lecture had been printed wrong. The lecture was just over. People were streaming away from the hall, looking disappointed.

Thasper and his friends were still in the street when the hall blew up. They were lucky not to be hurt. The police said it was a bomb. Thasper and his friends helped drag injured people clear of the blazing hall. It was exciting, but it was not the Sage.

By now Thasper knew he would never be happy until he had found the Sage. He told himself that he had to know if the reason behind the

Sage's questions was the one he thought. But it was more than that. Thasper was convinced that his fate was linked to the Sage's. He was certain the Sage *wanted* Thasper to find him.

But there was now a strong rumor in school and around town that the Sage had had enough of lectures and bomb attacks. He had retired to write a book. It was to be called *Questions of Dissolution*. Rumor also had it that the Sage was in lodgings somewhere near the Road of the Four Lions.

Thasper went to the Road of the Four Lions. There he was shameless. He knocked on doors and questioned passersby. He was told several times to go and ask an invisible dragon, but he took no notice. He went on asking until someone told him that Mrs. Tunap at No. 403 might know. Thasper knocked at No. 403, with his heart thumping.

Mrs. Tunap was a rather prim lady in a green turban. "I'm afraid not, dear," she said. "I'm new here." But before Thasper's heart could sink too far, she added, "But the people before me had a lodger. A very quiet gentleman. He left just before I came."

"Did he leave an address?" Thasper asked, holding his breath.

Mrs. Tunap consulted an old envelope pinned

to the wall in her hall. "It says here, 'Lodger gone to Golden Heart Square,' dear."

But in Golden Heart Square, a young gentleman who might have been the Sage had only looked at a room and gone. After that Thasper had to go home. The Altuns were not used to teenagers, and they worried about Thasper suddenly wanting to be out every evening.

Oddly enough, No. 403 Road of the Four Lions burned down that night.

Thasper saw clearly that assassins were after the Sage as well as he was. He became more obsessed with finding him than ever. He knew he could rescue the Sage if he caught him before the assassins did. He did not blame the Sage for moving about all the time.

Move about the Sage certainly did. Rumor had him next in Partridge Pleasaunce Street. When Thasper tracked him there, he found the Sage had moved to Fauntel Square. From Fauntel Square, the Sage seemed to move to Strong Wind Boulevard, and then to a poorer house in Station Street. There were many places after that.

By this time Thasper had developed a nose, a sixth sense, for where the Sage might be. A word, a mere hint about a quiet lodger, and Thasper was off, knocking on doors, questioning people, being told to ask an invisible dragon, and bewildering his parents by the way he kept rushing off every evening. But no matter how quickly Thasper acted on the latest hint, the Sage had always just left. And Thasper, in most cases, was only just ahead of the assassins. Houses caught fire or blew up, sometimes when he was still in the same street.

At last he was down to a very poor hint, which might or might not lead to New Unicorn Street. Thasper went there, wishing he did not have to spend all day at school. The Sage could move about as he pleased, and Thasper was tied down all day. No wonder he kept missing him. But he had high hopes of New Unicorn Street. It was the poor kind of place that the Sage had been favoring lately.

Alas for his hopes. The fat woman who opened the door laughed rudely in Thasper's face. "Don't bother me, son! Go and ask an invisible dragon!" And she slammed the door again.

Thasper stood in the street, keenly humiliated. And not even a hint of where to look next. Awful suspicions rose in his mind: he was making a fool of himself; he had set himself a wild-goose chase;

the Sage did not exist. In order not to think of these things, he gave way to anger. "All right!" he shouted at the shut door. "I *will* ask an invisible dragon! So there!" And carried by his anger, he ran down to the river and out across the nearest bridge.

He stopped in the middle of the bridge, leaning on the parapet, and knew he was making an utter fool of himself. There were no such things as invisible dragons. He was sure of that. But he was still in the grip of his obsession, and this was something he had set himself to do now. Even so, if there had been anyone about near the bridge, Thasper would have gone away. But it was deserted. Feeling an utter fool, he made the prayer sign to Ock, ruler of oceans—for Ock was the god in charge of all things to do with water—but he made the sign secretly, down under the parapet, so there was no chance of anyone seeing. Then he said, almost in a whisper, "Is there an invisible dragon here? I've got something to ask you."

Drops of water whirled over him. Something wetly fanned his face. He heard the something whirring. He turned his face that way and saw three blots of wet in a line along the parapet, each about two feet apart and each the size of two of his hands spread out together. Odder still, water was dripping out of nowhere all along the parapet, for a distance about twice as long as Thasper was tall.

Thasper laughed uneasily. "I'm imagining a dragon," he said. "If there was a dragon, those splotches would be the places where its body rests. Water dragons have no feet. And the length of the wetness suggests I must be imagining it about eleven feet long."

"I am fourteen feet long," said a voice out of nowhere. It was rather too near Thasper's face for comfort and blew fog at him. He drew back. "Make haste, child-of-a-god," said the voice. "What did you want to ask me?"

"I-I-I—" stammered Thasper. It was not just that he was scared. This was a body blow. It messed up utterly his notions about gods needing men to believe in them. But he pulled himself together. His voice only cracked a little as he said, "I'm looking for the Sage of Dissolution. Do you know where he is?"

The dragon laughed. It was a peculiar noise, like one of those water warblers people make bird noises with. "I'm afraid I can't tell you precisely where the Sage is," the voice out of nowhere said.

"You have to find him for yourself. Think about it, child-of-a-god. You must have noticed there's a pattern."

"Too right, there's a pattern!" Thasper said. "Everywhere he goes, I just miss him, and then the place catches fire!"

"That, too," said the dragon. "But there's a pattern to his lodgings, too. Look for it. That's all I can tell you, child-of-a-god. Any other questions?"

"No—for a wonder," Thasper said. "Thanks very much."

"You're welcome," said the invisible dragon. "People are always telling one another to ask us, and hardly anyone does. I'll see you again." Watery air whirled in Thasper's face. He leaned over the parapet and saw one prolonged clean splash in the river, and silver bubbles coming up. Then nothing. He was surprised to find his legs were shaking.

He steadied his knees and tramped home. He went to his room, and before he did anything else, he acted on a superstitious impulse he had not thought he had in him and took down the household god Alina insisted he keep in a niche over his bed. He put it carefully outside in the passage. Then he got out a map of the town and some red stickers and plotted out all the places where he had just missed the Sage.

The result had him dancing with excitement. The dragon was right. There was a pattern. The Sage had started in good lodgings at the better end of town. Then he had gradually moved to poorer places, but he had moved in a curve, down to the station and back toward the better part again. Now, the Altuns' house was just on the edge of the poorer part. The Sage was *coming this way!* New Unicorn Street had not been so far away. The next place should be nearer still. Thasper had only to look for a house on fire.

It was getting dark by then. Thasper threw his curtains back and leaned out of his window to look at the poorer streets. And there it was! There was a red and orange flicker to the left—in Harvest Moon Street, by the look of it. Thasper laughed aloud. He was actually grateful to the assassins!

He raced downstairs and out of the house. The anxious questions of parents and the yells of brothers and sisters followed him, but he slammed the door on them. Two minutes' running brought him to the scene of the fire. The street was a mad flicker of dark figures. People were piling furniture in the road. Some more people were helping a dazed woman in a crooked brown turban into a singed armchair.

"Didn't you have a lodger as well?" someone asked her anxiously.

The woman kept trying to straighten her turban. It was all she could really think of. "He didn't stay," she said. "I think he may be down at the Half Moon now."

Thasper waited for no more. He went pelting down the street.

The Half Moon was an inn on the corner of the same road. Most of the people who usually drank there must have been up the street, helping rescue furniture, but there was a dim light inside, enough to show a white notice in the window. ROOMS, it said.

Thasper burst inside. The barman was on a stool by the window craning to watch the house burn. He did not look at Thasper. "Where's your lodger?" gasped Thasper. "I've got a message. Urgent."

The barman did not turn around. "Upstairs, first on the left," he said. "The roof's caught. They'll have to act quick to save the house on either side."

Thasper heard him say this as he bounded upstairs. He turned left. He gave the briefest of knocks on the door there, flung it open, and rushed in.

The room was empty. The light was on, and it showed a stark bed, a stained table with an empty mug and some sheets of paper on it, and a fireplace with a mirror over it. Beside the fireplace another door was just swinging shut. Obviously somebody had just that moment gone through it.

Thasper bounded toward that door. But he was checked, for just a second, by seeing himself in the mirror over the fireplace. He had not meant to pause. But some trick of the mirror, which was old and brown and speckled, made his reflection look for a moment a great deal older. He looked easily over twenty. He looked—

He remembered the Letter from the Unknown. This was the time. He knew it was. He was about to meet the Sage. He had only to call him. Thasper went toward the still gently swinging door. He hesitated. The letter had said call at once. Knowing the Sage was just beyond the door, Thasper pushed it open a fraction and held it so with his fingers. He was full of doubts. He thought, Do I really believe the gods need people? Am I so sure? What shall I say to the Sage after all? He let the door slip shut again.

"Chrestomanci," he said miserably.

There was a *whoosh* of displaced air behind him. It buffeted Thasper half around. He stared. A tall man was standing by the stark bed. He was a most extraordinary figure in a long black robe, with what seemed to be yellow comets embroidered on it. The inside of the robe, swirling in the air, showed yellow, with black comets on it. The tall man had a very smooth dark head, very bright dark eyes, and, on his feet, what seemed to be red bedroom slippers.

"Thank goodness," said this outlandish person. "For a moment I was afraid you would go through that door."

The voice brought memory back to Thasper. "You brought me home through a picture when I was little," he said. "Are you Chrestomanci?"

"Yes," said the tall, outlandish man. "And you are Thasper. And now we must both leave before this building catches fire."

He took hold of Thasper's arm and towed him to the door which led to the stairs. As soon as he pushed the door open, thick smoke rolled in, filled with harsh crackling. It was clear that the inn was on fire already. Chrestomanci clapped the door shut again. The smoke set both of them coughing, Chrestomanci so violently that Thasper was afraid he would choke. He pulled both of them back into the middle of the room. By now smoke was twining up between the bare boards of the floor, causing Chrestomanci to cough again.

"This would happen just as I had gone to bed with flu," he said, when he could speak. "Such is life. These orderly gods of yours leave us no choice." He crossed the smoking floor and pushed open the door by the fireplace.

It opened onto blank space. Thasper gave a yelp of horror.

"Precisely," coughed Chrestomanci. "You were intended to crash to your death."

"Can't we jump to the ground?" Thasper suggested.

Chrestomanci shook his smooth head. "Not after they've done this to it. No. We'll have to carry the fight to them and go and visit the gods instead. Will you be kind enough to lend me your turban before we go?" Thasper stared at this odd request. "I would like to use it as a belt," Chrestomanci croaked. "The way to Heaven may be a little cold, and I only have pajamas under my dressing gown."

The striped undergarments Chrestomanci was

wearing did look a little thin. Thasper slowly unwound his turban. To go before gods bareheaded was probably no worse than going in nightclothes, he supposed. Besides, he did not believe there were any gods. He handed the turban over. Chrestomanci tied the length of pale blue cloth around his black and yellow gown and seemed to feel more comfortable.

"Now hang on to me," he said, "and you'll be all right." He took Thasper's arm again and walked up into the sky, dragging Thasper with him.

For a while Thasper was too stunned to speak. He could only marvel at the way they were treading up the sky as if there were invisible stairs in it. Chrestomanci was doing it in the most matter-of-fact way, coughing from time to time and shivering a little, but keeping very tight hold of Thasper nevertheless. In no time the town was a clutter of prettily lit dolls' houses below, with two red blots where two of them were burning. The stars were unwinding about them, above and below, as if they had already climbed above some of them.

"It's a long climb to Heaven," Chrestomanci observed. "Is there anything you'd like to know on the way?"

"Yes," said Thasper. "Did you say the gods are trying to kill me?"

"They are trying to eliminate the Sage of Dissolution," said Chrestomanci, "which they may not realize is the same thing. You see, you are the Sage."

"But I'm not!" Thasper insisted. "The Sage is a lot older than me, and he asks questions I never even thought of until I heard of him."

"Ah yes," said Chrestomanci. "I'm afraid there is an awful circularity to this. It's the fault of whoever tried to put you away as a small child. As far as I can work out, you stayed three years old for seven years—until you were making such a disturbance in our world that we had to find you and let you out. But in this world of Theare, highly organized and fixed as it is, the prophecy stated that you would begin preaching Dissolution at the age of twenty-three, or at least in this very year. Therefore the preaching had to begin this year. You did not need to appear. Did you ever speak to anyone who had actually heard the Sage preach?"

"No," said Thasper. "Come to think of it."

"Nobody did," said Chrestomanci. "You started in a small way anyway. First you wrote a book, which no one paid much heed to—"

"No, that's wrong," objected Thasper. "He—I—er, the Sage was writing a book *after* preaching."

"But don't you see," said Chrestomanci, "because you were back in Theare by then, the facts had to try to catch you up. They did this by running backward, until it was possible for you to arrive where you were supposed to be. Which was in that room in the inn there, at the start of your career. I suppose you are just old enough to start by now. And I suspect our celestial friends up here tumbled to this belatedly and tried to finish you off. It wouldn't have done them any good, as I shall shortly tell them." He began coughing again. They had climbed to where it was bitterly cold.

By this time the world was a dark arch below them. Thasper could see the blush of the sun, beginning to show underneath the world. They climbed on. The light grew. The sun appeared, a huge brightness in the distance underneath. A dim memory came again to Thasper. He struggled to believe that none of this was true, and he did not succeed.

"How do you know all this?" he asked bluntly.

"Have you heard of a god called Ock?" Chrestomanci coughed. "He came to talk to me when you should have been the age you are now.

He was worried—" He coughed again. "I shall have to save the rest of my breath for Heaven."

They climbed on, and the stars swam around them, until the stuff they were climbing changed and became solider. Soon they were climbing a dark ramp, which flushed pearly as they went upward. Here Chrestomanci let go of Thasper's arm and blew his nose on a gold-edged handkerchief with an air of relief. The pearl of the ramp grew to silver, and the silver to dazzling white. At length they were walking on level whiteness, through hall after hall.

The gods were gathered to meet them. None of them looked cordial.

"I fear we are not properly dressed," Chrestomanci murmured.

Thasper looked at the gods, and then at Chrestomanci, and squirmed with embarrassment. Fanciful and queer as Chrestomanci's garb was, it was still most obviously nightwear. The things on his feet were fur bedroom slippers. And there, looking like a piece of blue string around Chrestomanci's waist, was the turban Thasper should have been wearing.

The gods were magnificent, in golden trousers and jeweled turbans, and got more so as they approached the greater gods. Thasper's eye was caught by a god in shining cloth of gold, who surprised him by beaming a friendly, almost anxious look at him. Opposite him was a huge liquid-looking figure draped in pearls and diamonds. This god swiftly, but quite definitely, winked. Thasper was too awed to react, but Chrestomanci calmly winked back.

At the end of the halls, upon a massive throne, towered the mighty figure of Great Zond, clothed in white and purple, with a crown on his head. Chrestomanci looked up at Zond and thoughtfully blew his nose. It was hardly respectful.

"For what reason do two mortals trespass in our halls?" Zond thundered coldly.

Chrestomanci sneezed. "Because of your own folly," he said. "You gods of Theare have had everything so well worked out for so long that you can't see beyond your own routine."

"I shall blast you for that," Zond announced.

"Not if any of you wish to survive," Chrestomanci said.

There was a long murmur of protest from the other gods. They wished to survive. They were trying to work out what Chrestomanci meant. Zond saw it as a threat to his authority and thought he had better be cautious. "Proceed," he said.

"One of your most efficient features," Chrestomanci said, "is that your prophecies always come true. So why, when a prophecy is unpleasant to you, do you think you can alter it? That, my good gods, is rank folly. Besides, no one can halt his own Dissolution, least of all you gods of Theare. But you forgot. You forgot you had deprived both yourselves and mankind of any kind of free will, by organizing yourselves so precisely. You pushed Thasper, the Sage of Dissolution, into my world, forgetting that there is still chance in my world. By chance, Thasper was discovered after only seven years. Lucky for Theare that he was. I shudder to think what might have happened if Thasper had remained three years old for all his allotted lifetime."

"That was my fault!" cried Imperion. "I take the blame." He turned to Thasper. "Forgive me," he said. "You are my own son."

Was this, Thasper wondered, what Alina meant by the gods blessing her womb? He had not thought it was more than a figure of speech. He looked at Imperion, blinking a little in the god's dazzle. He was not wholly impressed. A fine god, and an honest one, but Thasper could see he had a limited outlook. "Of course I forgive you," he said politely.

"It is also lucky," Chrestomanci said, "that none of you succeeded in killing the Sage. Thasper is a god's son. That means there can only ever be one of him, and because of your prophecy, he has to be alive to preach Dissolution. You could have destroyed Theare. As it is, you have caused it to blur into a mass of cracks. Theare is too well organized to divide into two alternative worlds, as my world would. Instead, events have had to happen which could not have happened. Theare has cracked and warped, and you have all but brought about your own Dissolution."

"What can we *do*?" Zond said, aghast.

"There's only one thing you *can* do," Chrestomanci told him. "Let Thasper be. Let him preach Dissolution and stop trying to blow him up. That will bring about free will and a free future. Then either Theare will heal, or it will split, cleanly and painlessly, into two healthy worlds."

"So we bring about our own downfall?" Zond asked mournfully.

"It was always inevitable," said Chrestomanci.

Zond sighed. "Very well. Thasper, son of Imperion, I reluctantly give you my blessing to go forth and preach Dissolution. Go in peace."

Thasper bowed. Then he stood there silent a long time. He did not notice Imperion and Ock both trying to attract his attention. The newspaper report had talked of the Sage as full of anguish and self-doubt. Now he knew why. He looked at Chrestomanci, who was blowing his nose again.

"How can I preach Dissolution?" he said. "How can I not believe in the gods when I have seen them for myself?"

"That's a question you certainly should be asking," Chrestomanci croaked. "Go down to Theare and ask it." Thasper nodded and turned to go. Chrestomanci leaned toward him and said, from behind his handkerchief, "Ask yourself this, too: Can the gods catch flu? I think I may have given it to all of them. Find out and let me know, there's a good chap."